A NOTE ON THE AUTHOR

Megan Hastings was born in the Yorkshire Dales and grew up on a farm. She has since spent a year in Marburg Germany, teaching English as a foreign language, and has a degree and a Masters in Creative Writing. She works for the small charity, Active Impact, and facilitates writing workshops. Megan still lives in Yorkshire with the naughtiest guide dog, three guinea pigs, and her wonderful husband.

*A Referendum on Debra and Other Planet*s is her first novel.

A Referendum on Debra & Other Planets

Megan Hastings

write side left

ISBN: TPB: 978-1-7396993-6-9
ISBN:eBook: 978-1-7396993-7-6

Compilation & Cover Design by S A Harrison
Published by WriteSideLeft UK
https://www.writesideleft.com

A Referendum on Debra & Other Planets

Megan Hastings

Planet Poland

October 2015

Jacob likes being at school. Now, he knows lots of things he didn't know before. Yesterday he found out about Poland.

"How far away is Poland?" he asks his parents.

"Why do you want to know that, darling?" says Mummy.

"Poland." Daddy puts down his toast and picks up his phone. "Google says that Cheltenham is nine hundred and seventy-nine miles from Warsaw as the crow flies, so that would be the most direct route."

Jacob doesn't know what miles are. The trouble with his parents is that Mummy never answers his questions properly and Daddy's answers are too long.

"How is he supposed to know where Warsaw is?" Mummy says.

Jacob gets that small feeling when Mummy and Daddy talk about him like he's not there. He stops eating his Frosties.

"I'm sure he can work it out," says Daddy.

Mummy looks at Jacob.

"You're not eating your breakfast." She touches his forehead. "You haven't got a temperature, have you?"

"Oh for God's sake," says Daddy. "He's fine, aren't you, son? You just want to know about Poland."

Jacob nods.

"We haven't got time for this," says Mummy. "You've got to get ready for school."

Jacob nods because Mummy's face has gone all wrinkly. It's like Daddy's clothes the time that Mummy forgot to put them under the hot thing. Jacob wants to know if Mummy's face went under the hot thing, would it go flat like Daddy's clothes? When he had asked Daddy why bread isn't wrinkly and why the toaster doesn't make it flat like the clothes, Daddy told him so much about how bread is made that Jacob's head hurt.

"Let him have his question answered," says Daddy, like he always says when Jacob wants to know something, "or you'll be wondering about Poland all day, won't you, son?"

Jacob nods.

"Warsaw is the capital of Poland," Mummy says.

"But why do crows go there?" says Jacob.

"What?"

"You said crows fly there."

"As the crow flies means the most direct way of getting there," says Mummy. "Crows couldn't actually fly there, It's probably too far for them."

Jacob decides that Poland must be further away than Mars.

§

Jacob's new friend Marcin is from Poland.

"What's Poland like?" Jacob asks at playtime.

"It's really fun," Marcin says. "We go there every year and see my Aunty and Uncle and cousins. We play games and stuff. Daniel showed me how to juggle."

"But how do you get there?"

"We go on the plane and zoom up in the air like a space rocket."

"I haven't been on a plane," Jacob says.

Marcin shows Jacob what an aeroplane is like. He throws his arms out wide and whirls round and round. Jacob joins in. Spinning round and round is fun. Jacob can feel the playground spinning and the earth spinning too. Daddy says that the earth spins all the time. Jacob thinks this is strange because the earth only turns when he spins around. He wants to see if he can spin as fast as the earth but he falls over and nearly misses the ball Marcin throws to him.

"Good catch," says Marcin as Jacob grabs it with the tips of his fingers. "Let's play football."

"But we haven't got enough people," says Jacob.

Marcin leads him into part of the playground he hasn't been to before. This is the part where the biggerer children play. Jacob stays close to Marcin. The boys in this part are biggerer than him and they can shout louder than he can, even when he did the screaming competition last playtime.

"My brother will play with us," says Marcin, "and his friends. They like football."

Marcin's big brother is called Jarek. He's tall and he looks strong. Jarek says he will play football with them, and his friends play too. They run around very fast and Jacob hopes they won't run into him. He watches Jarek run after the ball and make super saves. He tries to copy Jarek but his legs aren't long enough.

§

"Why can't I have a brother?" Jacob asks his parents.

Mummy looks at Daddy.

"Would you like that, Jacob?" she says. "To have a little brother or sister?"

"Not a little one," says Jacob. "A big one. A big brother like Marcin's got."

Daddy laughs. "I don't think that's possible, son."

Jacob doesn't like it when Daddy laughs at him. "Why not?"

"Because," Daddy says. "Your mummy and I…"

"Because you were born first," says Mummy, talking over him.

Mummy always tells Jacob off for interrupting. When Daddy doesn't tell Mummy off, Jacob points his finger at her. "You're not supposed to interrupt," he says.

Daddy laughs again and Mummy's face goes all wrinkly. Jacob is just going to leave the room when Daddy says: "Tell us about Marcin, then."

"He's my friend." Jacob is still cross that Daddy laughed at him.

"Tell us more," says Daddy.

"No," says Jacob.

"Jacob, don't be silly," says Mummy.

"Leave him, Sash. Don't pander to him. Let him work through his sulks on his own."

Jacob doesn't know why Daddy says he is a panda. He has seen pandas on the telly. They are black and white and furry and live a long way away. He thinks about being a super strong panda and wants to know if pandas can play football.

"Tell us about your new friend, Jacob." Mummy is smiling at him. He likes it when Mummy smiles, it makes him feel like when he goes to bed with a hot-water bottle and gets a bedtime story.

"Marcin is the coolest. He's been on a plane, and he says it's like a space rocket, and he has a big brother called Jarek and we played football, and Marcin says I can go and play at his house on Friday."

"That sounds nice," says Mummy.

"But I don't want to."

"Why not, darling?"

Jacob doesn't know how to say the small feeling about being in strange places. He has seen Marcin's mum in the playground. She's very tall with a big loud voice. Jacob thinks she's a giant like the one in Jack and the Beanstalk. He wants to ask Marcin if she is a giant but he knows he shouldn't.

"It's good that you've made friends," says Mummy. "Why don't you want to go to his house?"

Daddy stands up to go. "Let him figure things out for himself," he says.

"He'll end up with no friends if he doesn't spend time with them outside school."

"He will in his own time."

Jacob stops listening like he does when his parents argue. He knows that it's best to stay quiet and think about something else. What if Marcin's house is as big as his mum? What if it's a giant house and he gets lost and...

"Why don't you want to go?" says Mummy again.

"I just don't want to," he says.

§

The best thing Jacob likes about school is when they all sit on the carpet and Mrs Thompson reads them a story.

"This book is called *Meg on the Moon*," she says.

Jacob leans in closer, going to the moon sounds exciting. Mrs Thompson starts the story, but Jacob finds it hard to listen because Marcin is wriggling around next to him.

Mrs Thompson stops reading and looks at Marcin. "You're very excitable today," she says. "Have you got the Friday feeling?"

"Jacob's coming to play at my house after school," says Marcin.

Jacob looks up. "Am I?"

"Yeah," says Marcin. "My mummy talked to your mummy, and she said you could. I can show you my football cards and my DVDs and you can have a go on my skateboard."

"That's very exciting," says Mrs Thompson, "but now, I want you to sit quietly."

Jacob can't listen to the story any more because he has a bad feeling in his tummy.

Jacob is behind Marcin when they walk out into the playground. Marcin is biggerer than him, just a little bit, so they are the same size when Jacob stands on tiptoes. He is making himself smaller by crunching down just a little bit. Now he can see over Marcin's head but if the giant can't see very well from up in the sky, Marcin's mum won't see him. He looks around all the parents. He wants Mummy to be there, even if she has a wrinkly face.

"There's Mamusia," says Marcin, pointing to the very tall woman.

Jarek is already standing with her. He grins at Jacob.

They walk home and Marcin's mum says, "How was school today?"

Jarek tells her about getting ten out of ten on his spelling test.

"That's so good," says Marcin's mum.

Jacob walks next to Marcin and tries to look like Marcin looks.

"And I nearly got all my sums right," says Marcin.

"That's great also," says Marcin's mum. "Maybe you will get them all right next time." She smiles at Jacob. "And how was your day, Jacob?"

He doesn't know what to say. He wants to hold Marcin's hand but he knows he mustn't be a baby.

"I'm going to show Jacob my bedroom," says Marcin.

Jacob is glad that he doesn't have to say anything now.

"Our bedroom," says Jarek.

"Your very messy bedroom," says Marcin's mum.

It's strange to walk a different way from school. It gets so narrow that Jacob has to walk behind Marcin and not next to him. There are lots of branches hanging over the fences and lots of big green bins so they have to go on the road to go past them. Mummy always tells him to be careful on the road but Marcin's mum just walks on the road and they go after her. Mummy always tells him to hurry up. She says she has lots to do and wants to get home quickly. Marcin's mum stops when Jarek wants to read the street signs.

"Marle Hill Road," Jarek reads.

"That's right," says Marcin's mum. "Not far now."

"I can read what our jumpers say," says Marcin. "They say Dunalley Primary School on them."

"You just know because someone told you," says Jarek. "You can't read it."

"Yes I can."

"Can't."

Marcin's mum does a big sigh like Mummy does. Jacob waits for her face to go wrinkly.

"If you can't read it now, you will be able to soon," she says to Marcin.

Marcin runs on ahead and Jarek reads the next sign.

"Brunswick Street," he says.

"Very good," says Marcin's mum.

"That's where we live," Marcin calls to Jacob and runs to a brown door. "This is our house."

Jacob and Jarek run after him. Jarek gets there first. Their mum comes last. Marcin stands on tiptoes to look at the silver number on the door. "It says two and an eight."

"Twenty-eight," says Jarek.

Magda smiles at them and turns the key in the door. Jacob follows Marcin inside.

The hall is very small with lots of coats all hung up in a jumble. Mummy makes every coat go on a different peg. Marcin's house doesn't smell like his house. Jacob's house smells like the bit of the supermarket where they have soap on the shelves. Marcin's house smells of flowers. Jacob goes to take his shoes off.

"Don't worry about that," Marcin's mum says. "You can leave your shoes if you want."

Mummy says no shoes in the house. Jacob doesn't know what to say.

Marcin's bedroom is biggerer than Jacob's and he shares it with Jarek. They have so many toys that Jacob doesn't know what to play with first. There are toys all over the floor, like he has them before Mummy tidies up. There's a giant Lego tower That's as tall as the bed.

"Don't touch that," says Marcin. "That's Jarek's. Everything on that side is his. Look at what I got for my birthday."

Marcin is holding out what looks like two plastic cups on both ends of a long spring. Jacob takes one of the cups and boings the other one through the air.

"That's not what you do," says Marcin. He takes hold of the other cup. "Look, it's a space phone. Put your ear in the cup."

Jacob feels silly holding the cup against his ear.

"Hello Jacob, this is Marcin the Martian." His voice sounds strange, like the Daleks in *Dr Who*, like he really is a Martian. "The spring makes it sound all wobbly."

"I want to do it," says Jacob, putting his cup over his mouth. "We can play space men."

Jarek runs in and jumps on his bed. "You're playing with that thing again."

"We're Martians," says Marcin. "Will you play with us?"

"Yeah, but we're not being Martians. We're always Martians."

"That's not fair," says Marcin.

"You have to think of a different planet."

Marcin glares at Jarek. "All the other planets are boring."

"It doesn't have to be real."

"Like Planet Sludge?"

"Boring," says Jarek.

Jacob has an idea. "Planet Poland," he says.

"Yeah," says Marcin. "Planet Poland."

Jarek is laughing. "Poland's not a planet."

"You said it didn't have to be real," Marcin says.

"But only two people can use the space phone," says Jarek, "so You're the English explorer."

"No, I'm from Planet Poland. You're the English explorer."

Jarek and Marcin start shouting at each other. Jacob doesn't know what the words mean. He thinks he knows what they're saying but he can't join in. He gets that feeling when Mummy and Daddy talk like he's not there.

Marcin's mum comes in. "What's this noise?"

Jacob feels better. Maybe Marcin's mum is a good giant who rescues him from the small feelings.

"Boys, what have I told you about speaking Polish with people who don't speak it?" she says.

Jarek and Marcin look at her and then look away.

"It's unpolite. You're being rude to Jacob because he doesn't know what you're saying." She smiles down at Jacob and puts a tray of milk and biscuits on the floor next to him. Then she goes out of the room.

Jarek comes over and shoves a biscuit into his mouth. Jacob takes one too. They are wafer biscuits and when Jacob puts one on his tongue, it goes into yummy chocolate sludge. He takes another and another. "I haven't had these before."

"They're just grzeski," says Marcin.

"We brought them back from Poland," says Jarek.

"Wow!" says Jacob.

Jarek and Marcin look at each other. Jacob thinks he really wants a brother to play with.

Planet Poland is a great game. They take turns being the English explorer. The explorer tries to zap the aliens on Planet Poland. Jarek is a really evil explorer. He wants to destroy the planet but Jacob and Marcin battle him back into his spaceship and blast him with super space guns. All too soon, Jacob hears Marcin's mum calling.

"Oh no! It's the horrible giant," he says.

Marcin laughs.

"Your mum must be here," says Jarek. "Quick, hide in the wardrobe." He shoves Jacob in with the hanging clothes and scrambles in after him.

Marcin jumps in too. His elbow keeps nudging Jacob's arm; it makes him giggle.

"Shshshsh," says Jarek.

They all start giggling. Then, Jacob hears Mummy

and Marcin's mum walk right past the wardrobe. He holds his breath and shuts his eyes and thinks very hard that Mummy and Marcin's mum won't find him.

"I don't know what they've been doing," says Marcin's mum. "Lots of running around the house, shouting about aliens."

Mummy calls Jacob's name again and again.

When they open the door, they will look in and not see anything and say, "Where have they gone?" but they will never know because they have disappeared like Meg and Mog when they went to the moon. Going to the moon, he will take his dinosaur jigsaw and his colouring book even though he has done most of it and the socks with trains on and Snowball and Daddy's phone so he can watch Arthur and Rugrats. Maybe he can really go to the moon but Mummy is still calling "Jacob! Jacob!" louder and louder and the spaceship can't take off even though He's the captain and they are trying very hard. They have to get away…

"Wait," says Marcin's mum in a behind-the-door voice. "I think I know where they are."

The door opens and Mummy and Marcin's mum peer in. Jacob keeps his eyes hard closed. If he can't see them, maybe they can't see him.

"Found you," says Marcin's mum.

Jacob goes with Jarek and Marcin out of the wardrobe.

"What have you been doing?" says Mummy. "Why were you hiding, Jacob? I've been calling you for ages."

"We're Martians," says Jacob.

"Well, what do you say to Magda, Jacob?"

"Thank you for having me, Mrs Marcin's mum," Jacob says.

"Oh, you're so nice." Marcin's mum bends down and gives Jacob a big hug. Her arms are strong, it makes him feel safe. "Call me Magda," she says and stands up again. This time, she doesn't seem so tall. "Which planet were you on today then?" she asks.

"Planet Poland," says Jacob.

Mummy looks at him. She opens her mouth like she's going to say something but she doesn't.

"Planet Poland!" says Aunty Magda.

She looks at Mummy and they start laughing. Jacob feels like when he spins round and round. Mummy doesn't laugh very much and he has said something funny.

§

After that, Jacob goes to Marcin's house a lot. Marcin and Jarek come and play with him too. Sometimes they play after school and sometimes they play when they don't have to go to school. One day, they all go to Sanford Park for a picnic. When they are playing and Jacob has to be quiet – like when it's his turn to hide, or when he's waiting to jump out on the boys – he hears the grown-ups talking downstairs. He hears Daddy and Uncle Stan, and Aunty Magda is always talking. Jacob likes it best when Mummy laughs. When Mummy laughs, Jacob closes his eyes and pretends he is zooming up into the sky in a tiny spaceship that carries him towards Planet Poland.

Moving In

March 2012

Sasha couldn't understand why Mike had bought the plants. He told her that he had stopped at Blooms on his way to work and had seen just the thing for the garden.

"Why didn't you wait until we were in the new house?" said Sasha.

Mike explained that he had been taking advantage of a special offer, and that he would drop his purchases off at the house before they moved the rest of their things. However, the plants had continued to live in the boot of Mike's car so that he now had to fit the boxes in around them.

Their new home was a simple two-up, two-down. Sasha had insisted that they needed an easy-to-manage house in which to bring up their son. Mike said that it should have a big garden for Jacob to play in. He liked things that weren't easy to manage, things that took up a lot of his time. Gardening or IT-related things and Mike would be focused for days. Anything else was fine with him, Sasha thought, as long as he didn't have to do it.

Most of the furniture had been transferred to their new house the day before. A van would arrive later with the rest, leaving Mike and Sasha to drive their last carload of things – baby stuff, bits from the kitchen, and Mike's precious plants – the short trip across Cheltenham. It took them most of the day to pack because someone always had to watch the baby. Eventually Jacob lay down in one of the empty boxes and fell asleep, leaving an exhausted Sasha to help Mike load the car.

§

It was late afternoon before they took a last look around the bare living room.

"It feels strange to be leaving," Mike said. "We've had some nice times here, haven't we?"

Sasha looked down into the last cardboard box. Jacob was still asleep. Mike held out his arms and she almost fell into them with weariness.

"I'm sorry you're so tired." He still smelt of the aftershave he had worn when they were dating.

"I used to love staying here," Sasha said. "It felt like a holiday home away from my flatmates."

Mike's reply was lost in Jacob's whimper to wakefulness. They broke apart.

When Sasha left the flat with Jacob in her arms, she groaned aloud at the number of boxes crammed into the car. A large plant pot took up most of the back seat.

"There's nowhere to put the car seat," Sasha said.

Mike looked up. "Oh. I forgot about that."

"How could you forget?"

"Perhaps he could sit on your lap. It isn't far."

"That's against the law," said Sasha, "and we've still got to put the car seat somewhere."

Mike began to unpack the car onto the pavement. Sasha tried to make it entertaining as she watched him fail to get everything back in.

"Look at Daddy," Sasha said, "Isn't he silly?"

Mike turned to her. "Well, I've got the car seat in."

"But your precious plant pot's still out here," said Sasha. "Two car trips it is, then." She strapped Jacob in, wanting to make a definite move towards leaving.

"Or… could you hold it for me, Sash? It won't be for long."

Sasha looked down at the plant pot. It contained a large pink rose. "That thing's massive!"

"Sorry, Sash. I'll drive slowly."

As Sasha opened her mouth to argue, her head gave a particularly painful throb. She felt too tired and threw herself into the front seat. "Put it by my feet, then."

"I don't want it to get knocked," said Mike, placing the rose on her lap.

Sasha swore. "Times Past," she said, reading the label aloud.

"Hold it tight," he said. "It's delicate."

The plant was heavy as well as large. Its pot dug into her legs and the petals tickled her nose.

"Why did you buy this stupid thing?"

"You're right," said Mike, reversing out of the driveway they had lived on for the last five years. "I should've waited. It'll look good when I've planted it out, though. I'm going to put it by the gate."

Jacob had fallen asleep as soon as they had left Millbrook Street. Sasha hoped they would be able to unpack the car without him waking. After five minutes of bad-tempered silence, Mike put on the radio.

"The economy has been given a major boost, with figures showing that exports outside of the European Union hit a record high," said the news reader. "This is due to increased trade to Russia, China and the United States."

"Turn it down," said Sasha. "I don't want the baby to wake up."

"Wait," said Mike. "Let me hear this."

"Tory MP Philip Davies claims that future economic growth is in markets outside of the EU. This has triggered fresh calls for Britain to leave the European Union altogether."

"I'm sick of the EU," said Sasha. "That's all we ever hear about these days."

"It's pretty important stuff," said Mike. "They're so fixated on money. It's peace I'm worried about."

Sasha snorted and switched off the radio. "Why's the traffic so shit?" she said as they came to a standstill once more.

"It's Race Week." Mike glanced at the car's display, "and it's five o'clock, so they're all coming out." He covered Sasha's hand with his.

Mike's fingers were clammy but she knew that this was his way of trying to make amends. Sasha resisted the urge to push him away for an uncomfortable minute before the lights changed and he moved his hand back to the wheel.

She knuckled her forehead. Trust them to move house during Race Week.

Jacob stayed asleep as they lugged their boxes into the new house. The thought of unpacking made Sasha's headache worse than ever. She rummaged in her handbag for paracetamol but could find only the empty packet. Mike was unloading the first few boxes. Sasha looked up as he let out a shout of pain.

"What's up?" she asked.

"It's all right, dropped a plant pot on my foot." Mike was saying something else, but the rest of his words were masked by Jacob's crying.

"Can you get him?" she called.

"In a minute," said Mike. "I just want to bring the fridge stuff in."

Sasha's hunt for painkillers was forgotten in the rush to rescue the baby from the hot confines of his car seat.

Even when the car had been unloaded and Jacob's every need had been attended to, he wouldn't settle.

"If you want a meal tonight," Sasha shouted over the screaming, "you'll have to take him off me."

She wished Mike could intuit these things without her having to delegate tasks. Sasha was so used to doing the organising that it had become hard-wired.

Mike had his hand in one of the boxes but he was staring out at the garden. "It's depressing out there."

Sasha came up beside him and thrust the baby at him.

Mike sat Jacob on his lap.

"Now, listen to me, son," he said. "Mummy and I are very busy, so we would appreciate it if you could keep quiet for a while."

"I'm surprised he can hear you over the noise he's making," Sasha said.

"Jacob, look… Come and look out of the window. No one's taken care of that garden for months."

"Stop him screaming."

"You heard your mother, Jacob."

"Treat him like a child for once."

Mike began to jiggle the baby and the volume of his crying decreased. "Someone's let mint grow wild," Mike said. "Look at it, choking those tulips. It'll have to go."

Sasha looked out into the dark bleakness of the new garden. The lawn was a mass of waist-high weeds. Some of the plants had grown too big for their stems to support them and they flopped across the path. She couldn't see any sign of a tulip.

"I'll put a pizza in," she said.

"I can't wait to get started on it," said Mike. He turned the rusty key to the door and stepped outside with the baby in his arms.

§

Although she had an early night, Sasha slept late the next morning. She rolled over to look at the clock on her bedside table, but there was no bedside table. When she got out of bed, Sasha's feet landed on floorboards instead of the sheepskin rug. When she entered the living room,

Sasha saw all the boxes waiting to be unpacked.

Mike was sitting amongst them, playing with Jacob and sipping a mug of coffee that was balanced on the end of a bookshelf. "Morning, Sash."

"Haven't you done any unpacking?"

"I've been talking to Jacob," Mike said. "I wanted you to have a good sleep."

"Thanks." She sat down beside him and took a drink of his coffee. She pulled out her phone and brought up Facebook. Emily had shared another cat video. The cat brought a ball back for its owner, its tail wagging. "That's so cute," Sasha said. "Look at this."

Mike leaned in to watch. "That's weird. It's panting like a dog, that can't be healthy."

"Cute though." Sasha scrolled down the page. 'Predictors of a Marital Storm: Experts Reveal Habits that could Sink a Marriage.'

"Why're you reading the *Daily Mail*?" said Mike.

"I'm not."

"You're on their website."

"I just read it on Facebook."

Mike gave her a look.

"Can't I sit down and check my Facebook for five minutes?" she said.

Mike yawned. "Well, now you're up, I was hoping to get on with the garden."

"What, and live in this mess for the rest of our lives?"

Just then, Jacob threw out a chubby fist and knocked over the coffee. He screamed as hot liquid ran onto his arm.

Sasha grabbed him. "Quick, get some water."

"It wasn't that hot," said Mike. "It's just a shock. You'll be all right, son."

"Then do something about this." Sasha pointed to where brown liquid seeped through a crack in one of the boxes and pooled on the floor.

Mike pulled back the coffee-stained cardboard. The bedroom curtains, a wedding present from Sasha's grandma, were now damp and stained.

Sasha's head was starting to ache again. "I can't do this," she said. "I don't know where any of the cleaning stuff is."

"I'll do it," said Mike.

Sasha held Jacob close, rubbing her face in his downy hair.

"I'll find some bleach or something, don't worry," Mike said.

"Bleach!"

"Or something."

Mike's approach to finding the cleaning things was to empty every box he found until he came to the right one.

"Watch where you're putting those cushions," said Sasha. "Let me do it."

Before long, Sasha had located the cloths and blotted away the coffee. She would have to get the curtains washed at a launderette. "All done." She looked up. Mike wasn't there. "Mike?"

"I've put Jacob in his cot and taken the monitor off charge." His voice sounded far away. "I'm going to start on the garden."

Sasha looked around at the mess Mike had made. "Don't bother to clear up any of this, will you?" she shouted and headed for the front door.

§

Slamming out of the house was therapeutic, Sasha thought. She resolved to do it more often. By the time she had walked around Clarence Square, however, she felt miserable. Sasha found herself back where she had started: standing in front of her new, dark green front door. She was considering slinking back and apologising to Mike when the door across from her opened.

"Everything all right?" The speaker was an aproned, plump woman.

"Yes, thanks," said Sasha. "I was just…"

"New, aren't you? I saw you move in last night. I'm Debra by the way, Debra Jackson. And you are? Actually, let's not stand around chatting out here." Debra lowered her voice. "You never know who might be listening. Come in."

Sasha followed Debra into her house, which smelled of baking and scented candles.

"I've just made fairy cakes," Debra said, "for the grandchildren, you know? We'll sample them, shall we?" She beckoned Sasha to a chair and pushed the plate of cakes towards her. "Take one. You look upset."

"Well…"

"Don't say it, moving stress. Tell me about you, then."

"Um, I'm Sasha…"

"You've moved in to number twenty-two, haven't you? Was that your husband carrying the baby? He's a handsome chap."

"Yes. Mike's my husband and my son, Jacob, He's just turned one."

"Ah. You do look wound up." Debra took a cake and slid the plate even closer to Sasha.

"Mike… sometimes, he just doesn't get it." Sasha picked from the plate and bit into an airy sponge. She closed her eyes as chocolate butter cream oozed over her tongue.

"I know what you mean, Sasha. My husband can't remember my name half the time! You've got a nice house, though. This is a good place for a boy to grow up."

Sasha had selected another cake without realising what she was doing. She held it to her face, breathing the sweet, icing sugar smell.

Debra was smiling at her. "Have as many as you like," she said. "As I was saying, we're nice around here. I mean, there was that burglary last Saturday but we think we know who did that." Debra continued in a loud whisper: "Mr Antisocial at number forty-three. His music's always on too loud and you only see him go out after dark." She gave Sasha a meaningful look. "Benefits." She got up to boil the kettle. "It's strange living here. It's hard to know what's going on with people. See what I mean?"

The last pulpy remnants of fairy cake felt like cardboard against Sasha's teeth. She yearned for Mike's familiarity and straightforward manner. Would he be looking for her?

"I'd better go."

"Sure you won't stay for a cuppa? You know what they say? Absence makes the heart grow fonder and all that."

Sasha stood up. "You'll have to come round when we're sorted."

"I'd love to." Debra showed her to the door. "If you ever need anything – babysitting services, cake, a shoulder to cry on – I'm only across the way."

"Thanks." Sasha smiled in what she hoped was a friendly way. She wasn't sure what to make of her new neighbour.

§

When Sasha got back, the house appeared to be empty. She ran upstairs and found Jacob chewing his hands in his cot. When he saw her, he smiled at her through the bars. She picked him up, feeling an intense sense of love and being loved. "Let's go and find Daddy," she said.

Sasha stopped still in the doorway to the garden.

"Almost finished," Mike said, straightening up from behind the wheelbarrow.

Sasha gazed at the cleared path with its trimmed border. Patches of bright flowers now showed where the weeds had been.

"Those gaps won't be there for long," Mike said, pointing them out to her. "I'll buy some things to plant there this afternoon."

Sasha didn't know what to say, but she knew that Mike could read her approval. As she moved further into the garden, she thought she could smell lavender and hear the drone of contented insects close by.

"Good thing we moved in the Spring," Mike said.

Sasha looked from his earth-stained jeans to the leaves clinging to his t-shirt and up into the familiar softness of his face. He was standing in front of their garden gate, which was now framed by the pink rosettes of Times Past. She moved Jacob onto one hip and when she held out an arm, Mike stepped into the hug.

The Proposal

February 2008

It began on one of those evenings when Mike and Sasha folded themselves into the sofa with a tube of Pringles between them. Mike had put on the Six Nations – England versus France – a choice that Sasha wasn't keen on until he reminded her that this was what everyone else would be watching. She was looking at the screen but her frequent Pringle-munching and phone-checking conveyed her lack of interest.

"Do you know what day it is on Friday?" Sasha asked.

Wilkinson had just made a spectacular tackle.

"Mike?"

"Mmm?"

Without looking, he knew that she had taken another crisp; she would hold it between salty finger and thumb for several seconds before nibbling at an edge.

"Friday." Mike tried to pay attention to their conversation by visualising his small leather-covered diary. Although he had started to put most of his appointments in his phone, his diary was the first place he checked.

"There's nothing on the calendar."

Sasha was still holding the Pringle. "I meant the date."

"Friday. That would be the 29th."

"Exactly. It's a leap year."

Mike wasn't sure what to say to that. In any case, this was an exciting match.

When it was over, they were down to the dust at the bottom of the Pringles tube. Mike was about to tip out the last few crumbs when Sasha uncrossed a slippered foot and nudged the tube onto the floor. She shifted along the sofa and pulled his arm around her. "You know what they say about leap years?" Her voice was muffled against his shoulder.

"I don't know, you tell me." To distract himself from the tightening in his throat he experienced whenever they had this type of conversation, Mike buried his hands in her fine hair and curled it around his fingers like gift ribbon.

"It's the one day when the woman gets to propose." Sasha jerked her head upwards, pulling her hair free. Her expression was that mixture of flirtation and severity that charmed him in the way it attracts most men. "So, unless you can find the right moment in the next few days, you might find me asking you, Michael Glanford."

§

It wasn't the first time they had talked about marriage. Sasha had been dropping hints for the last few months. He already knew that she wanted to get married in the village where she grew up and that she wanted her bridesmaid to wear the royal blue dress she had spotted online. Mike knew that he wanted to marry her. He had learnt to read Sasha as easily as if she were a piece of software. Over the years, he had become so skilled at avoiding disagreements between them that they rarely argued. He couldn't imagine spending his days with anyone else. Yet the thought of marriage made him anxious. When Sasha had first mentioned her dream ring, Mike's throat had dried up. Marriage was a big thing. She had described the dresses and all the other wedding details so frequently and factually that Mike now just accepted that they would marry. His next worry had been about making his vows and the after-dinner speech; he hated public speaking. He decided that Dutch courage would have to get him through. For now, the one thing that really terrified him was the thought of making that proposal.

§

On Sunday morning, Mike left a sleeping Sasha and went out to buy the dream ring. He was glad that she had mentioned its price because he never kept large amounts in his current account. The bank transfer had been made and a piece of paper was wrapped around his card with details of its product number and Sasha's ring size. Mike had only taken a few steps inside H. Samuel when he spotted the display. Rings. More rings than he had ever seen in his life. They glimmered and twinkled, scattering the light into thousands of eye-watering fragments. He made his way to the counter in the gloom left by the absence of the rings. Mike fumbled for his wallet and thrust the crumpled piece of paper at the woman behind the counter.

"So that's the white gold one-carat Forever Diamond Ring?" she asked.

Mike nodded; it was as if she had spoken a different language.

"White gold is nice but it can lose its shine after a few years," said the assistant. "Are you sure she wouldn't prefer yellow gold? Rose gold is lovely too."

"No, that's the one she wants."

"Ah, so she already knows about this, does she?" The woman laughed her salesperson laugh. "This should be about what you want too. I mean, this is about both of you."

Mike thought that what he really wanted was to get out of the shop. "I just want her to be happy."

"Good answer. And, before I get your ring out of the cabinet for you, would you like to add a Premier Care insurance plan? It means that you can bring the ring back for any repairs and we can replace it in the event of accidental damage, theft, that kind of thing."

Mike dithered. He hadn't even thought about insurance.

"Considering how much you're paying for the ring, it would only be adding a small cost in the grand scheme of things."

"No thanks. I'll take out my own policy."

"If you're sure. I'd hate anything to happen to it in

the meantime." She disappeared and came back with the boxed ring.

Mike put his card into the machine and paid the four-figure sum without looking at the amount on screen.

As he drove home, the ring in its box was as hard and uncomfortable in his pocket as the thought of asking his girlfriend those four important words. Mike didn't have an easy relationship with words. He found that, when he wanted to say something important, their meaning deserted him. He wondered about having a drink to calm his nerves, but Sasha would smell the alcohol on him. She would be unhappy that his proposal hadn't been made sober. Mike hid the ring in his briefcase, the one place he could be sure Sasha wouldn't look. The box nudged his hand every time he opened his briefcase that week and in between meetings, Mike wondered how, when and where he was going to do it.

§

On Tuesday, he picked up the phone before he could change his mind and booked a table at one of their favourite restaurants. He felt as if he had run a marathon when the arrangement had been made. Mike texted Sasha to tell her. Her happiness flooded back across his phone's screen: a long line of xs and smiley faces. Mike was proud of himself. He would do it that night.

It had been the first dry evening for a long time. The wind had dropped and Sasha said that it felt like the beginning of something spring-like.

"I heard that we're going to have the hottest February on record."

Mike laughed. "You said it was going to snow yesterday."

"Yeah, well, that's what they said on the news." Sasha linked her arm through Mike's. "We'll walk to Gianni's, shall we?"

Mike breathed in the cool, crisp air. The walk took away the tension of his day at work so that they both arrived happy and refreshed. The restaurant was quiet. Mike ordered drinks and looked at Sasha opposite him. She had taken off her coat, revealing a dress that was patterned in the colours of a peacock's tail feathers. The hair he so loved to tangle had been tied back from her small face. It was a lovely evening, Mike thought, as the waiter poured their wine. The boxed ring was a small pressure against his leg. He took a sip of Cinzano and then another. Now was a good time. As Sasha told him about an amusing email she had received that afternoon, Mike moved a hand towards his pocket. He tried to put a finger inside to lever out the boxed ring but the space was too narrow. It hadn't felt that tight when he had put the ring there an hour before. He wondered if it was to do with the way he was sitting and shifted position without looking away from Sasha.

"Have you decided what you would like to eat?" The waiter was back.

They ordered and relaxed again into being themselves.

"Why do you always go posh when you order?" Mike asked, still trying to release the ring.

"Do I?" Sasha looked surprised and laughed. "What do I sound like? It must be because I used to do this, you know? I used to think that the people who sounded nice were the ones that deserved good service. I bet I sound awful."

"Actually," Mike looked into her eyes, "I think it makes you sound rather charming."

Sasha took Mike's hand across the table. He hoped sweat wasn't gathering on his palm; he was starting to feel hot. "Sasha?"

There were few people in the restaurant but the thought of going down on one knee with the waiters around was agonising. Could he propose without going down on one knee? This would be a moment they would remember forever. He didn't want to fail Sasha. She was waiting for him to say something. "Sasha... I... Did you see the news about Boris Johnson?"

Sasha looked surprised; she had no more idea of what he had been about to say than he had. Why couldn't he do the right thing?

"You mean about him being Mayor of London?" said Sasha.

"Yep," said Mike. "I'm so glad I got out of there."

"I kind of like him. That baby face is cute."

Mike took a drink of wine to hide his expression.

"And he's funny, don't you think?" said Sasha.

"He's just stupid," said Mike. "How he got into politics... He's now saying that he'll let motorbikes use the London bus lanes. That's gone down really well."

"Well it would, if you're a motorcyclist."

"If I were a motorcyclist," said Mike, "I would only take the bike out after dark where no one would see me driving around like a twat." He thought this would make Sasha laugh.

"My dad had a motorbike," she said. "I loved riding around in the sidecar. I hoped we could do that together, one day."

Mike wished that conversations wouldn't run away with them and twist the mood into something that closed Sasha off from him.

He was saved by the arrival of their food. Sasha ate quickly, but by now Mike was so on edge that it was difficult to swallow.

He paused and put down his fork. "Sasha?"

She smiled at him, her eyes questioning – her way of nudging him into saying the right thing this time.

The ring felt heavy in his pocket.

"Spit it out then." She was laughing.

"I… I really love you, you know?"

§

When Mike got up to leave two hours later, he felt as if he had experienced another day in the office. Sasha wouldn't stop smiling at him, a sign, Mike knew, that she was upset by his lack of proposal and didn't want to spoil their evening by letting him know that. Mike became more physically affectionate to communicate that he was aware of his failure. He wanted to prolong the evening, to have another chance.

"We could go for a walk in Pittville Park," he said.

"In the dark and cold?" Sasha slipped her arm through his. "Why not?"

There was something special about the two of them walking in the dark. An owl called above them, and Sasha clung to Mike's arm.

"That sound always scares me," she whispered.

"You're not cold, are you?" Mike asked.

"No."

He pointed towards a bench that was illuminated by one of the orange lamps. "Shall we sit here for a bit?"

Sasha sank down and leaned against him.

Mike put his arm around her, swallowed, and reached for her hand. Soon, his girlfriend would be his fiancée. He could do this.

"Are you scared too?" Sasha asked.

"No. Why?"

"What's with the firm grip?"

Mike looked down at his fingers: thick and clumsy things hiding Sasha's dainty hands. He made to move away but her grip held him there. This was the right time to do it; there was no one around and the tranquillity was perfect. The minutes passed. Neither of them moved or spoke and Mike felt the moment slide out of his grasp as if he were watching his lives disappear in a computer game.

§

On Thursday, Sasha said that she would cook something nice that evening.

"I'll make something from that recipe book Mum gave me for Christmas," she said.

"Great," said Mike. "What were you thinking?"

"I'm not sure yet, but I'll make it good."

Sasha, who often came home from her nine-to-five receptionist job to do the cooking, the housework and sometimes the paperwork besides. Sasha, who could invent plausible excuses to explain Mike's absence from yet another family party. Yes, Mike thought, that was Sasha; she always made it good.

The ring was now back in his briefcase. Mike had to open it a lot that day. Each time he did, it was always the first thing he found. It was as if the ring were clamouring to escape its box and begin a new life on Sasha's finger. He had several large folders to put away before he could go to lunch and the last one stubbornly refused to slide in. Sure enough, he found the small jewellery box blocking the compartment. He had been haunted by the saleswoman's words about insurance and never let the ring go far from him. Mike transferred the ring to his jacket pocket, stuffed the folder in, and hurried away from his desk.

The grounds of Mike's offices were so luxurious that turning his back on them to go into the building felt like a betrayal. He always took his lunch break at the same time each day and walked alongside perfectly tended lawns and patchwork flowerbeds before coming to his favourite bench. Its wooden back was warm when the sun shone, and it was close to a herb garden. Mike unwrapped his sandwich and listened to the rhythmic thwacks of rackets from the nearby tennis court. When he had finished eating, Mike took the box out of his pocket. He opened it, wondering how such a small object could cause so much trouble. Even he could see that the ring was beautiful. It was topped with a cluster of diamonds that caught the light. Looking at it, Mike was reminded of being very small and lying by a river. He had watched the sun shine on the water and been fascinated by the wonder and brightness of it. He closed the box, the childhood memory forgotten.

§

Mike could smell roasting chicken as he entered the flat. It made a refreshing change from the greasy odour of fry-ups that the students in their block were forever making. Mike breathed deeply and detected a faint whiff that reminded him of the herb garden – thyme, perhaps.

"Chicken breast wrapped in mozzarella and bacon," Sasha told him.

By the time he had changed out of his suit, the table had been laid and rosé poured. This felt easier than being out in public, Mike decided. Sasha was wearing a thick cardigan that she often wore for cooking. Mike had changed into his baggy house-trousers; their pockets were so big that he kept having to touch them to remind himself that the ring was still inside. He would have no problem producing it today. As they ate, they talked about normal things: their days at work, the car's MOT, Emily and Michelle coming on Sunday. All the time, Mike felt they were going through the motions. He knew they were both wondering if it would be today. At last, he could stand it no longer.

He put his knife and fork together. "Sasha?"

She chewed slowly, looking at him in amusement. She swallowed. "Go on then."

"Sasha… Sasha, will you marry me?"

§

"We're thinking of having the wedding in June next year. The twenty-fourth of June. We're having it at my parents' place. I can't believe we're engaged!"

Engaged. Mike wasn't sure how he felt about it. Any sense of victory at having finally asked the question had been quashed by the weariness at having Sasha talk of nothing but the wedding.

"I just can't believe it," Sasha said again, although their relationship status on Facebook had been the first thing to change.

Mike went into the living room, where Sasha was talking to her two friends.

"Congratulations, Mike!" Emily swooped over and kissed him before he was even through the door.

He smiled and tried to hug her in a way that didn't look awkward.

"Sash has been telling us all about it," Emily said. "It sounds amazing. The dress looks fab, and that ring!"

Sasha waved her hand so that the ring winked at Mike, sending a bright shaft of light his way. As he crossed to a chair, he caught Michelle's eye. She was less of an extrovert than the other two girls and just then, Mike felt that he was sharing something with her.

§

Mike was glad when they had the flat to themselves again. He flopped on the sofa and patted the space beside him. "Let's see what's on tonight then."

"Oh." Sasha hadn't joined him. "I wanted to get the invites drafted and I need to start writing a list of things to do."

Mike channel-flicked for half an hour, admired the paper Sasha shoved under his nose, and headed upstairs. He and Sasha usually went up at the same time. Mike lay in the cold double bed and waited for sleep to come.

In the Middle

November 2012

Sasha and Mike each hoped to be the first to see their son walk. Sasha was sure she would witness his first steps; she was with him most of the time, after all. The bond she had created with Jacob was strong and one hundred percent rewarding.

Mike knew that his son was a daddy's boy. Although Jacob had his mother's curly blonde hair and freckles, Mike could already see the traces of hero worship in Jacob's eyes when he looked at his father. For Mike, Jacob's first wobbly steps would naturally lead to football, running around the park – things that he would teach his son.

If Sasha and Mike spent their time together with Jacob, they would have shared the joy of their son like birds guarding a nest. Instead, they squabbled. Mike felt Sasha was overprotective of Jacob but didn't know how to say this without upsetting her. The closest he had got was to tell his son:

"Your Mum worries about you ever such a lot. What do you think, Jacob?"

"You treat him like he's an adult," Sasha had said.

"He will be, one day," Mike replied.

Sasha was glad she had Debra to talk to.

"I just wish he'd hurry up and walk," Sasha said. "He's been this close for ages."

"I don't know why you're wishing his life away," Debra said. "Once he starts walking, you'll be in the middle of something and he'll be in the way all the time."

§

Mike wasn't the kind of person who confided his feelings. He had placed a photo of Jacob next to his computer – the one Sasha had taken of Mike pushing him on the swing. Mike looked at it a lot, his pride and love propelling him through office hours. Sometimes he would break off from whatever he happened to be in the middle of doing to look into his son's laughing face; many half-written emails had been left in his Drafts folder that way.

§

Mike and Sasha's evenings went like this: Mike took over with Jacob when he came back from work which meant that Sasha could have a nap before a night with the baby. Mike would return from putting Jacob to bed to find Sasha on the sofa, dopey with sleep and looking her most peaceful. He would sit beside her and they would hold hands. Most nights, they were too tired to do more than that but occasionally they talked softly, moving from the domestic things to remembering some of their first dates, their honeymoon, and the day trips they'd taken to beautiful parts of the Cotswolds.

"I love that model village," Sasha sighed one evening. "I wish we could live like that, all small and hidden away."

Mike was quiet for a while. "We could go to Bourton-on-the-Water this weekend."

"I doubt it's very pram-friendly," Sasha said, getting up from the sofa.

§

A few weeks later, Sasha had to go to the dentist for a filling. She asked Debra if she would mind looking after Jacob.

"Of course not," Debra said. "I've got the grandchildren here. It'll be nice for Jacob to have someone to play with for a change."

When Sasha returned from her ordeal – still light-headed from the gas and air and with a mouth that tasted of rubber – Debra was brimful of smiles.

"He did it!" she exclaimed, hugging Sasha on the doorstep. "It was almost like he copied my Emily. She's been taking little steps for a few months now. So I was holding her hands and she was walking to me and, what do you know? Jacob pulls himself up on Emily's walker and takes a few steps."

Sasha frowned. It made her face hurt. "He's never pulled himself up on anything that moves before. Is he all right?"

"Fine. Come in, come in. I've just taken a banana loaf out of the oven."

Sasha followed her inside. "So he didn't hurt himself?"

"Well, he came down on his knees but you know what they're like? All padding at that age."

Debra made for the kitchen but Sasha headed to the sitting room. Jacob was sitting in front of the telly with Debra's grandchildren. When he saw his mother, he crawled across the room and reached out to be picked up.

Sasha hugged him briefly before pulling Emily's walker towards her. "What's this?"

Jacob clung onto the walker but wouldn't let go.

"He'll do it in his own time," said Debra, coming in with a tray. "He's probably gone a bit shy."

Despite all Sasha's efforts as she ate banana loaf and chatted to Debra, she couldn't get Jacob to walk.

§

"He's done it," Sasha told Mike that evening.

"Started walking?" Mike said.

Sasha nodded.

"Did you get it on camera?"

"I didn't have time for that."

"You should've texted me," said Mike.

"I didn't want to disturb the latest project," Sasha said.

Mike felt a tired, heavy disappointment; Jacob had performed those first steps for his mother, after all. He fought to keep a good-natured appearance as he said: "Let's see, then."

Sasha helped Jacob pull himself up against the arm of the sofa. She hadn't had any more luck at getting him to walk than she'd had at Debra's but she wasn't going to tell Mike that. Jacob held on to the sofa arm as Sasha went to the end of the room.

"Come on, then. Come to Mummy."

Jacob looked at his mother but didn't move.

"Why don't you come and talk to me, Jacob?" said Mike from his kneeling position in the doorway.

Sasha felt a fierce need for her son. She could spend hours with him and still relish the feel of his light little body in her arms, his fuzzy head against her chest. Jacob smelt of baby lotion and a new scent that she couldn't quite name.

"Come and see Mummy." Sasha's plea was as desolate as a bird's call.

The small child looked from one parent to the other.

"Come on then," Sasha said again and Jacob let go.

Mike's day at work had been awful – so awful that he had tried to change his screensaver to a photo of Jacob eating chocolate mousse. Only when he came up against an error message did Mike remember that it had been he who had headed the previous summer's operation to put blocks in place to prevent staff from doing any such thing. After that, Mike had been in such a bad mood that he had kept Jacob's photo open and maximised his son's chocolate-smeared face to get through the remaining meetings.

Caught in the five o'clock rush hour, Mike had put on the radio. The news headlines did nothing to improve his mood: Iain Duncan Smith pressurising Cameron into a referendum; Russians marching through Moscow to protest against immigration, and something about some celebrity going through a divorce. Mike wondered what kind of world his son would grow up in. An intolerant one, judging by the Russians' performance. At last he was home, with his very real, very special son.

"Come and tell me about your day, Jacob," Mike said, holding out his arms.

Jacob looked at him, back to his mother, and then turned with wobbling lip to his father. Jacob's concentration failed and he fell on his bottom.

Outspoken

8 May 2015

Mike had been pleased to find that Gav Higgins was working on another of his projects. Gav had a cheerful round face and a work ethic that made him the most efficient Perimeter Security Officer Mike had ever met. He often spent most of the evening in the office, staring at computer screens, drinking unhealthy amounts of coffee and leaving only when the job was done. He would have irritated Mike if he wasn't such a laugh. Gav's wisecracks had kept him going through many a team meeting and his Project Boards were far easier to run with Gav on board. It hadn't taken Mike long to realise that staff socials were only worth going to if Gav was going.

Mike was about to join Gav on a call to fix a firewall issue with a piece of software. This particular package would upgrade the company's computers to a decent version of Windows. After three stop-start years, Mike had put it forward to go live the week before but for whatever reason the company's firewall was now blocking its own upgrade. They needed to dial into the Indian equivalent of their office to talk to the technician who would be working on the problem.

Mike called into the conference line. A tinny version of Vivaldi's Four Seasons played in his ear as he opened the spreadsheet that contained his notes. Mike was just wondering how long it would be before someone changed the dreadful conference tone when the music stopped.

"Morning, Mike." Gav was the first to join the call.

"How're you doing, Gav?"

"All right, thanks. A bit tired, I was here most of the night and then I decided to stay up to watch the election results."

"I went to bed," said Mike. "I saw the first few come in and felt like stuffing my head under the pillow."

"We're in safe hands now," said Gav. "That coalition seemed like a good idea but Cameron was always being held back. It's time he had a clear field."

Mike didn't reply. His hopelessness at the thought of a Tory government was too painful to share.

"Are we ready to call into the space station?" said Gav.

The Indian offices had a notoriously patchy signal.

"I think so," said Mike. "Are you all right to chair this one? That way, I can type up the notes."

"Chair it? How generous of you," said Gav.

Mike heard coffee being sipped down the phone.

"Excuse us," said Gav. "I can't chair without my coffee."

The line beeped, an indication that someone else had joined the call.

"Hello?" said Gav. Silence. "Anyone there?"

Mike's ear was filled with a mixture of crackles and background office noise.

"This… vi… em… all."

"Couldn't catch that, sorry," said Gav. "Is that Vijay on the line?"

In the silence that followed, Gav let out a long sigh. Mike guessed he had forgotten to mute his phone and hoped the line was too bad for Vijay to hear it.

"Yes, this is Vijay. I'm waiting… come… call."

"We have Mike Glanford on the line. Are we ready to start?"

Although Mike could see only the back of Gav's head from where he was sitting, he could visualise his fingers drumming impatient rhythms on his desk.

Background noise again.

"I'm… wait one minute… another technician… join us," said Vijay.

The line faded and then a beep.

"Do we have someone else on the call?" Gav asked.

"Yes, this is Vijay."

"Yeah, I know we have you, Vijay. I'm asking who's just joined us."

A voice barely audible over the sounds of people coming and going in a country far away. "I'm Vijay as well."

"The other technician… called Vijay. We are two Vijays."

"All right. So we have Vijay… the Vijay who first joined the call, I'll call you Vijay one. Is that all right?"

"I… uh… connect."

"It's just so we can differentiate between the two of you in the notes."

"Hang on," said Mike. "Vijay – the Vijay who first joined the call – your surname's Prasad, isn't it?"

"Yes."

"I'm not sure we have time for this," said Gav.

"I was just thinking that perhaps you could be Vijay P," Mike explained, "and Vijay, the one that's just joined us, can be…"

"Vijay one and two is easier," Gav said.

"So… saying… Vijay two?"

"I think so," said Gav. "Neither of you sound particularly clear. Any chance of a better line?"

"Sorry… connection… not good."

"All right," said Gav, cutting across the stilted apology. "Vijay one, I'll start with you. Could you give us an update on where we are with this firewall issue?"

"I don't understand… problem."

Gav sighed before speaking slowly and clearly. "What is it about the problem that you don't understand?"

"It… simple… de… wall… problem."

"What did you say?"

"Vijay… saying… easy to deactivate… firewall. Turn… off."

"Oh, I see," said Mike. "Yes, that occurred to us too."

"If it were as simple as just deactivating the firewall," said Gav, "why have I been here all night?"

Mike tried to keep his tone light and reasonable. "That's how it should work."

"Yeah, that's how it used to work before…"

"It's a good point, Vijay," said Mike. "However, they're unwilling to let us simply deactivate the firewall for the purposes of installing the upgrade."

"Think of the viruses we could be letting in," said Gav, "even for… however long it will take to install this thing."

"I see… problem."

"How far have you got with finding a solution?" Gav asked.

"Sorry?"

"After we spoke on Tuesday, you were going to go away and see what you could find out about…"

"Ah, yes… difficult… your firewall… different to… office here."

"So you haven't got anything for us, then?" said Gav.

"I keep looking… maybe… email… solution if…"

Beep.

"I think there's someone else on the call," said Mike.

Silence.

"Are you still there, Vijay… um, Vijays?" Mike asked.

"Still here," a voice came back.

"What about you, Vijay One or Two or whoever you are?" said Gav.

Silence.

"I think we… lost… Vijay."

"Which one?" Gav's voice had risen so much that Mike muted the volume switch on his headset. "Vijay one or two?"

"I don't know which Vijay I am."

§

Forty-five minutes of crackly, distorted conversation later and they had made progress. The technicians suggested where the fault might be and Gav had agreed to put it right within a matter of hours. They disconnected from the call. Mike was just about to put down the phone when Gav said:

"Isn't it typical? We have a simple fault with a massive project like this and we end up with two techies called Vijay!"

Mike sat back in his chair and started to laugh. "It does make it confusing."

"Vijay one and Vijay two… sounds even more like a space station."

"I hope our space stations have better communication than this," said Mike. "They'd never get off the ground otherwise."

He had hoped Gav would laugh but his joke seemed to have made him angrier.

"It's ridiculous. You can't hear what's being said most of the time, It's a wonder anything gets done."

Mike was still laughing. "And they call this progress," he said.

"It's not progress though, is it? In fact, it's a massive step back. What a waste of time. Talking to that lot is like trying to get blood out of a stone. That call should have taken half an hour max."

Mike had never seen Gav in a temper before. In these situations, he found that his best course of action was to try to inject some reason into the conversation. "It didn't take much longer."

"Too long when you have so much to do. Make sure you charge them the full hour, Mike."

"It'll take me that long to type up these notes," said Mike.

"And work out which flipping Vijay said what. Don't you think we were much better off when we did things ourselves instead of contracting all our work out to these third-party companies halfway across the world?"

"It saves us some work though," Mike said.

"Does it? Most of the time we end up running around after them, clearing up their mess because they've no clue what they're doing. It's like he said on the call just now. He didn't do the work for us because his firewalls are different to ours."

"A firewall's a firewall," said Mike.

"So he had no ex…"

"It's the systems that must be different."

"I'm only telling you what he said. He should have let us know beforehand that he didn't do the work."

"Most people don't these days," said Mike. "I swear communication's getting worse."

"Exactly, we should do things ourselves."

"I'm not talking about third parties," Mike continued, calmly. "I'm talking about us. Here. This place."

"I don't know. Sorry, Mike, I don't mean to moan, but I've been up with this problem most of the night and I swear it wouldn't have happened if we'd implemented the firewalls ourselves instead of handing it over to all the Vijays in Asia."

Mike tried to work out how their conversation had ended up like this. They had laughed about the call, and Mike couldn't wait for Gav to tell everyone about it at the staff meal on Friday. Gav always told a good anecdote, and they could all enjoy the ridiculousness of having two techies with the same name. Suddenly, the things Gav was saying had stopped being funny. He was sure that Gav wouldn't be saying this if they were talking face to face.

"I'm not sure…," Mike began.

"I'm not saying this because it's what I think. I'm saying it because it's what's best for business. Can't you see that we're better off without them?"

The line was once more silent. The lack of crackly bursts of communication should have been a relief, but to Mike the pause seemed eerie.

"Anyway, I'm making another coffee if you want one," Gav said.

Mike thought of Gav, sitting good-naturedly behind his desk, up for a chat with anyone who passed. Now, he realised how small Gav's world was behind his screen. If the two Vijays strolled by, would Gav offer them a coffee too? Mike felt tired, as if his first meeting of the day had lasted three hours instead of less than the allotted hour. The coffee would be hot and strong and would clear his head. Gav always added plenty of sugar to his cups and presented them to his colleagues with a couple of Jaffa cakes that were stashed in a desk drawer. Yet the coffee would be bitter too – as unsavoury to Mike's stomach as the things he had just heard his colleague say.

"I'd best get on," Mike said. He disconnected the call.

You In?

May 2016

When her neighbour appeared on the doorstep with another home-baked cake, Sasha felt obliged to invite Debra in. She would linger on the threshold as they talked about their families, the weather, and other matters trivial enough for the street to hear. After a few minutes of watching Debra balancing the Tupperware against her cardiganned bosom, Sasha would beckon her inside for tea and a slice of the cake. Today, however, Sasha was anxious to return to the garden. Debra was telling her about a coffee morning she had been to, but Sasha was thinking of her small son and the now unsupervised paddling pool.

In the back garden, Jacob splashed around with his playmate from school. They jumped from lawn to pool, pool to lawn so their shorts flapped in the slipstream.

"Be careful," Sasha called. "Don't fall."

Jacob ignored her and it was his friend, Marcin, who glanced up from his crouched position on the lawn.

"We won't." Marcin threw himself into the water.

Sasha joined Debra in the shade of the patio. "Boys."

"I have to say, I wouldn't like mine to be five again," said Debra. "Mind you, It's not much better when they're twenty-five. I've got my son nagging me to fill in his Student Finance application and Annie asking to borrow money for a mortgage."

Sasha tried to imagine a time when Jacob would be wanting money for a house. Thinking about it made her head ache.

"It's the paperwork that drives me mad." Debra's fat rolls wobbled, a familiar sign to Sasha that her neighbour was working herself into full rant mode. "All this stuff in the post. It took me five hours to fill out his finance application and they sent it back with corrections. Three times, three times I had to send it back. Cost me a fortune in stamps, they had to be first class as well. And I got another of those leaflets yesterday."

Sasha looked up. "Leaflets?"

"Vote Leave, you know?"

"Oh, those. I don't waste my time reading them."

"Me neither, I know which way I'm voting."

A jet of water soaked the back of Sasha's dress. She turned around so quickly that the boys' laughter rippled dizzyingly around her. Jacob had uncoiled the garden hose and was pointing the end at her.

Sasha marched over to the giggling culprits. "Put that away, now. It's dangerous."

Jacob stuck out his chin. "Squirting people isn't dangerous."

"If you fall over that hose or slip on a wet patch, you'll

be in hospital with a broken leg. Look what a mess you've made of the lawn."

Sasha wound up the hose and returned to the table. "Boys."

Debra was laughing. "What a telling off! You shouted loud enough for the whole neighbourhood to hear. Not that everyone round here would understand you, of course."

Sasha looked around and saw that the boys had returned to the paddling pool. "What do you mean?"

Debra leant towards Sasha as if imparting confidential information and asked if she had met the new people at number thirty-two. "I saw them yesterday in the street. He was carrying that baby and I waved, like a good neighbour should, but did he wave back?"

Sasha laughed. "It's hard to wave when you're holding a baby. You should know."

"But they didn't wave back."

Sasha thought that this was the trouble with Debra. She was apt to judge people on a single gesture. "You'll be saying they didn't like your Facebook post next."

"I wouldn't let them anywhere near my Facebook."

"He seems pretty high up. He works at GCHQ."

Debra slumped back in her chair. "Well, I'm surprised. I didn't think he could speak English."

Sasha said nothing. If she annoyed Debra, she knew that half the street would stop speaking to her.

Instead, she forced herself to listen to the lapping of water against the paddling pool's plastic rim. The boys chattered softly to one another like nesting birds. Jacob was less of a worry to her when he had a friend to keep him happy.

"What's he called then?" Debra's voice blocked out these gentler sounds.

"Who?"

"Jacob's little friend." Debra glanced at the boys, who had retreated to the far end of the garden.

"That's Marcin, Magda's son."

"Magda?"

"Magda Jankowska."

Debra shook her head.

"I thought you'd know her through the PTA. She's got so many people helping out with the fete now."

"Oh, that reminds me. I'll donate a cake or two and I'm sure I can sort out some bric-à-brac."

"That would be a big help. If you let Magda know, she'll come and collect it from you."

"I think I'll leave you to tell her if that's all right." Debra glanced around and lowered her voice. "I'm not very good with foreign accents."

The sun hung heavy and fierce in the sky. Sasha hoped the children hadn't heard what Debra had said. She stood.

"Is something wrong?" Debra asked.

Sasha's chest felt as if a winged animal were trapped behind her rib cage. "They might be getting sunburnt."

The boys came reluctantly. She rubbed sun lotion into their squirming bodies, careful not to miss an inch of their soft, damp skin.

Debra was watching Marcin.

"So where do you live, dear?"

When Marcin smiled at Debra, Sasha thought how many times she had seen that same smile on Magda's face.

"I live at twenty-eight Brunswick Street," Marcin said.

"That's nice. Have you always lived there?"

"Yes, but Jarek hasn't. He was born in…"

Jacob banged the table. "I want some lemonade."

"What do you say, Jacob?" said Sasha. "I'm waiting for the p word."

He stuck out his tongue. "Poo face."

The boys giggled.

When the children had run into the garden and were rolling about on the lawn, Sasha said: "I'm so sorry. Jacob's really showing me up today."

Debra was watching her. "You need a break."

Sasha wished she would look away. Debra's eyes, usually so sharp and calculating, now had a concerned look about them. Sasha thought it made her seem a lot older.

"When was the last time you had a night out?"

Sasha considered. "It wasn't that long ago."

"If you can't remember the date, it was too long ago. You know I'm always looking after the grandchildren and It's no bother if you want me to babysit one evening."

The doorbell rang and Sasha stood up.

She knew it was Magda by the hummed rendition of Pharrell Williams's *Happy*. Sasha could hear it halfway down the hall.

"Hey, lovely lady." Magda stood on the doorstep; her bangled arms open in greeting. "Let me in quick. People are staring."

Sasha could see Mrs Patterson peering out of her open window. She wondered if Magda had been dancing along with the humming. Her friend stepped inside, and they embraced. Sasha loved these hugs because, like everything Magda did, they were given with great energy.

"Sasha, you look so pretty today."

She glanced down at her crumpled dress, still damp from being squirted and stained with sun cream. "If you say so. Come through."

Debra was hunched over the garden table, looking at her phone.

Sasha sat down beside her. "Debra, this is my friend Magda. Marcin's mum."

"I've come to take my boy away. I hope he hasn't been a pain."

They watched the two boys running towards the house.

"Don't disappear," Sasha called but they were already out of sight.

Hiding was their favourite way of extending their play dates.

Sasha turned to Magda. "He's been fine. This is Debra."

"Ah, the one who makes the lovely cakes."

Debra didn't smile.

"I do my best."

Sasha looked at her. "You're too modest. How're the fete preparations going, Magda?"

"Oh, fine," said Magda. "Just a couple more volunteers and we've done it."

Sasha thought Debra would offer her services at this point. When she didn't, Sasha said:

"You'll bake something, won't you, Debra?"

Debra was looking at her phone again. "I'm not sure I could make that sort of cake."

Sasha couldn't understand this. Her time with Debra was always punctuated with platefuls of creamy Victoria sponge, tarts that flaked deliciously on the tongue and shortbread which filled the mouth with rich buttery warmth. Sasha couldn't think what to say and a heavy silence fell over them.

It was Magda who broke it. "I'm actually thinking of putting my scones in the baking competition." She was smiling but it looked like hard work. "If you wanted to enter too, we could make it a real contest."

Debra acted as if she hadn't heard Magda.

"So, how about it? Are you in?"

Debra's finger flicked left and right through the list of emojis on screen. "If I'm not too busy. I never know what I'm doing these days with my grandchildren to look after and all my other commitments."

"I understand that but if you did bake something, I can tell you it would sell like… do you say hot cakes?"

Sasha joined in with Magda's laughter. Then she saw Debra's face.

"I didn't think you would enter the competition." Debra said this in a rush.

"Why not?" said Sasha. "I'd put something in myself if my cakes didn't taste like cardboard."

"I thought she was organising it."

Debra didn't look at Magda.

"I'm sorting everything out behind the scenes." Magda was trying to catch her eye. "Don't worry, I won't be involved with the judging or anything."

"Isn't it a local contest?" said Debra. "My impression is that the fete is for people who are local to the school."

"Of course it is," said Magda, unsmiling.

Debra didn't say anything.

Sasha turned to face her. "Are you saying Magda's not local?"

Debra said nothing. Sasha stared at her. She couldn't believe that this was the same woman who waved to Jacob on his way to school and gave away so many of her things to charity. Sasha had known Debra to be less than complimentary about the neighbours behind their backs but she had never thought she could be so openly rude.

"Debra, Magda's lived here for eight years."

"Hey, let's not argue about cake," Magda said.

Sasha looked around. Magda was sitting back in her chair and staring at the table. Sasha had never seen her looking so unsure of herself.

"I bet your cake tastes amazing, but it is just cake." Magda tried to say this with her usual buoyancy.

"That's not the point." Debra's words hung in the quiet garden. In a nearby tree, a blackbird began to make its alarm call. "This isn't about cake, it's about our community. All those people from outside… You don't see neighbourhoods coming together any more."

"As I said, Magda's got a lot of people helping…"

"But it isn't the same if you're not from here."

Sasha was on her feet. Her hands were shaking so much that she had to curl them into fists to steady them. "If you really think that, Debra, you can leave my garden."

Debra stared at her in a rare moment of speechlessness.

"Go," Sasha said.

Debra looked at Sasha and Magda. Sasha was trying to decide what to say next when Debra stood up. She turned away and walked slowly across the lawn.

Sasha was beginning to let out her breath when Debra reached to open the gate and caught her sleeve on the rose that grew there. She seemed to take a long time to free herself. Sasha stayed where she was, looking on in detached amusement as her neighbour unpicked thorns from the delicate stitching.

Sasha sat down but didn't speak until the garden gate had creaked shut. "I'm sorry."

Magda touched her shoulder. "Hey, it's not your fault."

Sasha wanted to cry. She felt so drained that it was hard to look at Magda.

"I'm a big girl," said Magda. "I can look after myself. Trust me, I have thick skin."

"We got talking about the referendum. That's what this is really about."

Magda agreed that the upcoming referendum was creating an unpleasant atmosphere. She told Sasha about getting the bus into town a few days before and how she'd had to tell her children off for being noisy. "The way people were looking at me… it was worse than your neighbours."

"They were judging you for shouting at your kids?" Sasha asked.

"No. They were staring at me because I wasn't speaking English."

Sasha tried to reassure her friend by reminding her that not everyone thought that way. "There are some pretty stupid people around here," she added.

"I just laughed." Magda threw her head back, her laugh as warm and deep as the caramel sun. "You keep going, don't you, and hope you're not heading for a breakdown."

Sasha squeezed Magda's hand. "It'll all blow over in a few weeks. No one's going to vote to leave Europe, there's too much in it for us."

Magda rubbed a hand over her face as though to smooth out the frown lines. "We'd better find those boys."

They called them but got no response. Sasha went inside and looked in all the rooms. Everything was in its place: ordered and still. Even Jacob's Action Men stood in a line along his bedroom windowsill.

She came back out into the garden. "They're not here, are they?"

"No, it's much too quiet for that," Magda said.

They called the boys' names again but only the blackbird answered with its alarm call. Sasha followed Magda around the lawn, searching the flowerbeds and down the gap between the greenhouse and next door's fence.

"Do you think they're up there?" Sasha peered into her neighbour's apple tree.

"We'd see them if they were," Magda said.

Sasha felt as if there was something blocking her

airways. "I don't know where else to look." A pain flashed across her temple. "Where could they... They might be... What if they've... Do you think they're on the road?"

Magda put a hand on her arm. "You're very pale, Sash."

Sasha turned away and began to pace the lawn. "What if they're on St Paul's Road? It's such a horrible place to cross. They could get run over."

"Slow down, Sasha. They're not that stupid, they wouldn't go far."

"I have to look." Sasha went out onto the street and walked up and down with Magda close behind her. They looked in people's gardens and even behind bins but the boys weren't there.

§

Sasha had just resumed her anxious pacing of the garden when a door banged inside the house. The boys came out onto the lawn.

"There you are," said Magda.

"Where were you?" Sasha was shouting and crying at the same time. "We were calling, we were looking for you. I thought something awful..."

Jacob took several steps backwards and his bottom lip quivered.

"It's all right now," said Magda, "Just make sure that if you're going to hide, you don't leave the garden, okay?"

"We were hiding in the airing cupboard," said Jacob.

Sasha tried to smile. "That's where you were."

Marcin looked up at Magda. "Jacob showed me the hokey cokey."

"The what?"

"You put your right arm in, your right arm out."

Jacob joined in. "In, out, in, out, you shake it all about."

The boys were doing actions along with their raucous singing. "You do the hokey cokey and you turn around."

Sasha watched it happen. As Jacob span around, his foot slipped from under him and he came down hard on one knee. She saw his shock and then his face caved inwards with the pain. She needed to rush to her son, to scoop him into her arms and cradle his downy head against her aching heart. She stepped forward and put her arms out to him. Yet, before she could touch him, Jacob was standing again.

He bit his lip hard and a tear smeared his cheek. He put up a hand and blotted it away. Then he turned to Sasha. "I'm okay," he said.

In that moment, Sasha knew that her son was starting to need her less. Thoughts of his growing up had filled her with sadness, but that was before she had seen how tough he could be. Sasha watched the blackbird fly from the branches of the apple tree and disappear high over the cluster of houses that made up her street. In the quiet that was left behind, Debra's words came back to her: all those people from outside. She thought of the country Debra so clearly wanted England to become. An England severed from Europe's embrace – what kind of place would that be for her son? One day, Jacob would go out into the world and endure much worse than bruised knees, but for now, Sasha would make the most of being his mother.

Out on the Town

June 2016

It had been a long time since Sasha had struggled to choose which perfume to wear. Usually she sprayed on a bit of Happy before starting the day but now she stood in front of her dressing table, contemplating the jumble of bottles. Deep Night was at the front, its purple crescent made pink in the evening sunlight. This was the perfume Sasha wore for going to meetings and other school functions. Jacob said it made her smell like a strawberry. Sasha passed over it; she wasn't in a fruity mood. Tall and elegant, Sunflowers stood beside her moisturiser. She reserved it for family occasions after her mother had bought it three Christmases before.

A dusty bottle had been pushed to the back. Sasha picked it up and saw that it was Marc Jacobs Daisy. She took off the lid, which was modelled to look like a bunch of plastic flowers and breathed in its sharp scent. This was the perfume Mike had given her in their first year together. Back then their trips out, dinners in country pubs and long walks in the Cotswolds had been permeated with its seductive, summery smell. When Sasha was pregnant, her senses of smell and taste had worked in a different way. She discovered that bananas smelt like wet dogs and that pork really did taste of pig. Sasha had to hold her nose when loading the washing machine because it reeked of damp, dirty clothes. In those months, Daisy completely changed for Sasha. She could pick out its mellower base notes and a vague varnish-like scent which she suspected was some sort of binding ingredient. She loved the way that Daisy hung in her nostrils and cleared her head. After her morning shower, she would take deep sniffs from the bottle for a good couple of minutes before pulling herself together.

"You look like you're drinking it," Mike said as he dressed one morning.

"I can't help it. It's just so…"

"I'm sure it's normal," he said from under his towel.

Sasha sprayed her wrists. "How about Daisy for a girl?"

Mike laughed. "And Marc Jacobs for a boy?"

"Well, Jacob would be nice."

"I had an Uncle Mark, so we could use it as a middle name if you like."

"Jacob Mark Glanford." Sasha looked down at the bulge beneath her work suit. "That sounds good."

§

The Daisy bottle was cool in Sasha's hand. She looked down and saw that there was only a dribble of it left. She would have to press the spray again and again to get any out but Sasha couldn't quite bring herself to throw it away. She considered using the last of it now but that would be like having the shadow of a younger Mike with her all evening.

When she put the Daisy back, her hand brushed another bottle which had been half hidden by her make-up bag. She rolled it out, recognising the almost conical bottle as Killer Queen. Sasha had worn something similar at school. She had first smelt it on Emily at their year eleven prom – the night they had persuaded Michelle to take a sip of Malibu. Two glasses later and she was tipsier than even Emily had been. Turning her back on the dressing table, Sasha sprayed her wrist and inhaled the smell of adventure. Yes, this would do nicely.

Downstairs, Sasha lingered in the living room doorway. "I'm off now."

Jacob didn't look up from the television but Mike turned towards her.

"Remind me which restaurant you're going to?" He said this as if trying not to sound too interested.

"Zizzi. I shouldn't be back late. Jacob, I want you in bed by eight."

Her son, still staring at the TV, blew a loud raspberry. "Jacob!"

Mike sprawled on the sofa and looked down at Jacob. "Well, as it's Friday, I'm inclined to let you stay up a bit later."

"No, he can't," said Sasha. "It completely disrupts his sleeping pattern."

Jacob was grinning up at Mike.

"But only if you're good," Mike said to him.

Trust Mike to wind her up before her night out. "Just because you're never here to put him to bed. You don't have to deal with the tantrums."

Mike held up a hand. "All right, all right. I won't keep him up too late."

"Eight o'clock."

"Eight o'clock. You go out and enjoy yourself and stop worrying about Jacob."

"Bye then, Jacob," said Sasha.

Jacob didn't reply.

"Jacob, say goodbye to your mother, please," said Mike.

"Goodbye to your mother, please," Jacob said.

Sasha headed for the front door, thinking that her chance to get away hadn't come soon enough.

"Sasha?"

She paused.

"You look really…"

"I'm late, Mike."

She had her hand on the doorknob now.

"Sasha?"

"What?"

"Say hi to the girls for me."

§

Sasha had been looking forward to this evening ever since Emily had texted her a few weeks before. Emily was coming to visit her mother in Cheltenham and wondered if Sasha wanted to meet up. Michelle was free too and so the date had been set. The three girls had gone to school together and been in the same classes all the way through. Then they had separated; Emily and Michelle went to universities in Newcastle and Cambridge and Sasha went nowhere in particular. She had never wanted to go to university.

They were both waiting outside Zizzi. Emily bounced up to Sasha and leant in for a hug. "It's so good to see you."

"You too." Sasha looked over at Michelle.

She was standing a little apart from them, her serious face turned to Sasha.

"Hi Michelle." Sasha knew better than to hug her. She had once joked that Michelle was as physically affectionate as a lamppost.

They went inside and were soon ordering drinks. The waiter went to Emily first. Sasha was used to people deferring to Emily as the natural leader of their group.

"A Coke, please," she said.

Michelle looked taken aback but followed her lead and ordered a lemonade.

"The same for me," Sasha said. "Starting slowly tonight, are we?" She grinned at her friends, remembering when they had drunk far too much too quickly so that their time together was a fizzy giddiness that not even next day's pounding head could make her regret.

"You're not driving are you, Em?" Michelle asked.

"Oh no, I've left my car at Mum's. The one-way system is too nightmarish."

When they had chosen their food, Emily took a sip of her drink and said: "I've got something to tell you."

This was a familiar opening to Sasha. Emily was the kind of person who found a lot of things exciting and so "I've got something to tell you" always prefixed information on her latest crush, gossip about which girls had split up with boyfriends, and even the antics of their new puppy. The last time, it had been about her honeymoon in Majorca.

"Tell us then," Sasha said.

Emily took another drink. "Well, I... we... we're going to have a baby."

Sasha felt a rush of warmth that made her eyes water. "That's the best news."

"I expect Paul's pleased," said Michelle.

"Oh yeah, he can't wait to be a dad."

Sasha remembered Paul as he had been in his bridegroom's suit: radiating a boyish energy as he greeted his guests, yet fervent and honest when he made his vows. It had been a great wedding. She had watched the couple dance and only looked away when she caught Mike's eye. She laid her arms around him and steered her husband onto the dance floor. In that moment, there had been an unspoken knowledge between the two of them and Sasha realised that no one understood her in the way Mike did. In those days, he could spin her round and round without her getting dizzy. Then Jacob had come along.

"It's great feeling," said Sasha. "Being a mum is... Jacob's such a pain, sometimes I'd do anything to get rid of him for an hour but I don't think I'd change..." She found she couldn't continue.

Emily was crying too. "I've done all the crazy stuff, now I feel like I'm ready to give up the booze and be a mum."

As Sasha shook her head, she saw that Michelle's face had relaxed. She was bending forward into their conversation; it was what Emily called her "thawing out".

"No wine?" said Sasha. "I wouldn't rush into that."

"Raising a child in this difficult world," Michelle said, "You'll be needing it."

Emily was laughing. "Always the pessimist. It's not that bad."

"Let's see how it goes on Thursday," Michelle said.

"We are not talking about that this evening," said Sasha, just as their pizzas arrived.

The silence that fell when the waiter departed could have been because they were eating but Sasha felt she had shut down the conversation. She asked Michelle about her job and for the next ten minutes, she listened to her friend venting her managerial woes.

"I'm already looking forward to my maternity leave," Emily said, and they were back to talking about the baby.

Their plates were empty by the time they had exhausted the subject. In the lull before dessert, they got out their phones and showed each other pictures that hadn't made it onto Facebook. Sasha flicked through the photos of Jacob's fifth birthday party.

"Aww bless." Emily pointed at the image of Jacob's chocolate-smeared face. "He looks like mini-Mikey. They've got the same chin."

"How is Mike, anyway?" Michelle asked.

Sasha locked her phone and Jacob's face faded to black. "Oh, he's all right."

"Just all right?"

"Well, you know, Mike's Mike." She saw her two friends look at each other.

"I'm surprised you haven't told us what he's been up to," said Emily. "We couldn't get you to talk about anything else before you had Jacob."

"He's just working," said Sasha. "I want to see the pictures of your new place, Michelle."

Michelle showed them each room of her house. Sasha thought it looked cosy – small enough for one but big enough for the occasional guest.

"Of course, I'll be making some changes."

"It's gorgeous," said Sasha. "I love the colour of the kitchen walls, so sunny."

"Yeah, don't change anything," said Emily, "except get rid of some of those books and buy a Kindle like a normal person."

Michelle looked as if Emily had said something disgusting.

"When do you have time to read them all?" said Emily.

"It's the Cambridge in me," said Michelle, swiping to the next photo.

The image of her kitchen was replaced with a photo of a kitten running through long grass. The caption above it read "WE WILL KILL THIS KITTEN IF YOU VOTE TO BREXIT".

"Why is this on my phone?" said Michelle. "My friend WhatsApped it to me yesterday." She tapped the screen hard with one finger. "Delete."

"That kitten's adorable," said Emily.

Sasha said, "What've cats got to do with Brexit?"

Michelle was giving her a shrewd look, the same expression she wore when she had asked complicated questions of her teachers. "Why don't you want to talk about it then?"

Sasha took a deep breath, feeling pizza crumbs scratch her throat. "Because…" Sasha thought back to last week when she had forced Debra out of the garden. The picture of Debra's stunned face was sharp and raw. "Because I'm sick of it."

"But isn't it such an important moment for us?" Emily said. "It could be historical."

Sasha stared at her. Michelle was the one who got involved with campaigning and tried to talk others into her way of thinking. Over the years, neither she nor Emily had ever taken an interest in her political activities.

"It's also our present," said Michelle. "That's why this referendum is about what we do right now."

As Sasha reached for the water jug, a waft of Killer Queen rose from her wrist. The scent seemed incongruously sweet against the backdrop of Italian herbs. "Which is what?"

Michelle turned to Emily. "You know, sometimes I realise just how lucky I was to go to uni."

Sasha didn't understand this, but Emily replied:

"Yeah. I think you can only really, like, know what's going on now if you've lived and studied with people from all over the world."

"Thing is, people who haven't been to uni just don't have that experience of life."

Their puddings arrived. Sasha's first spoonful of

gelato was too cold. Her tongue felt clumsy and numb as she forced it to form the words that needed to be said. "I don't know. We terribly inexperienced people who missed out on university might even have a better grasp of the real world than you do."

Although Michelle turned her flushed face away, Emily was smiling at her.

"We weren't talking about you, Sash. You worked your arse off in that design company, even though they treated you like shit. Moving house with a baby and working part-time, I couldn't have done it."

Sasha said nothing. She felt trapped between these compliments and the argument that seemed to be pushing her two oldest friends away. Sasha thought of Magda with her hugs and her laugh, and how she calmly ploughed through life. She wondered what Magda would do if she were here.

"I guess you met people at uni who would be affected if we left Europe?" Sasha asked.

"My supervisor was French," said Michelle. "He was so intelligent, gave me a good mark too."

"There were a few foreign… like, European people in my class," Emily said.

Sasha remembered what Magda had said: you keep going and hope you're not heading for a breakdown.

"Yeah, it sounds like you really understand about Brexit," Sasha said.

She beckoned the waiter over and ordered a large glass of Shiraz. She almost laughed at her friends' looks of longing and felt triumphant when Emily asked for another Coke.

"And for you?" The waiter turned to Michelle.

She stayed silent. Sasha could feel Michelle's bookish, fact-heavy brain torn between her need to have a drink and her loyalty to Emily. "Nothing for me, thanks."

Emily had a strange look on her face – a mixture of apology and conviction. "What we meant is that when you go to uni, you learn so much about, you know, the world and why our country is the way it is."

Sasha was replying before she could stop herself. "Didn't you go nocturnal, drink a lot and ask your parents to bail you out with pocket money every month? I'm sure that taught you loads about the real world." Sasha's discomfort was reflected in her friends' miserable faces. "Can't we just change the subject?"

"I think you misunderstood what we were trying to say," Michelle said.

Their drinks came quickly. Sasha took long sips of the wine, the girls' envious looks enriching its taste.

"What I was trying to say," said Michelle, "is that it's what we do now that's important."

"Like, have a normal conversation?" Sasha ventured.

"Like vote," Michelle said.

"I've seen so many Facebook posts from people who say they won't be voting on Thursday," said Emily. "It's such a waste. I wish I could take all their votes and vote for them."

"I think it goes back to what we were saying about university," said Michelle. "A lot of people who won't be voting simply don't have that understanding."

Sasha tried to keep enjoying the wine but her anger

was making it difficult. She was determined to say something that would overturn her friends' assurance of their own superiority. She put down her glass. "I'm not going to vote."

Michelle stared at her.

"I'm not voting," said Sasha. "There are too many things we don't understand and too many sides to take – or should I say, avoid taking."

There was a strained silence in which Sasha finished the last of her wine and signalled to the waiter for more. To her disappointment, he didn't come over to see if her friends wanted anything.

"It's a personal thing," Michelle said, "but so many women fought hard to give us the freedom to vote."

Sasha took her fresh glass from the waiter. "They fought so we could have the freedom to choose whether to vote or not."

In the time it took Sasha to drink her wine, Emily got out her phone and began texting. Michelle was looking at Sasha without really looking at her at all. Sasha guessed she was trying to find a way to have the last word.

When the waiter asked if they wanted anything else, Emily hesitated before saying: "Just the bill, I think."

"And then we're off to Revs," said Sasha.

Michelle frowned. "Are we?"

"We usually do. I want one of those amazing cocktails."

"I'm not sure." Emily patted her belly. "I'm already starting to get tired."

"Exactly," said Sasha. "You have to make the most of doing these things before the kid comes along."

Emily didn't look convinced. "You drank that wine pretty quickly, Sash."

The restaurant was spinning but Sasha wasn't going to tell her friends that. "Just for one drink. Come on, let's make it like old times."

Sasha walked along the Prom a little ahead of the others. She breathed in the smells of warmed pavement and a rich meaty aroma from the nearby Café Rouge. Sasha's phone vibrated in her pocket. When she took it out, she saw "Magda" on screen. She stopped and the others stopped too. "Just a sec," she said, tapping the screen to answer.

"Hey Sasha. I need your help." Magda sounded calm but there was something forced about it.

"What's up?"

"I need you to look after the kids for me. Sorry, I'm not sure who else to ask." Her voice cracked.

"What, now?"

"Please. Stan's… Stan's in hospital."

"What?"

"He's been hurt. They told me he was attacked. I need to go to him."

Sasha didn't remember the rushed goodbye she said to her friends, nor the route she took to Brunswick Street. Her next memory was of Magda opening the door and giving her a brief mechanical hug.

"I have to go," Magda said. "I'll text you. I hope we won't be too long."

§

Sasha had spent a lot of time in this house but without Magda, the bright paintings and patchwork rug seemed to have lost their colour. Magda liked to burn jasmine oil; Sasha normally adored this exotic scent but now its strength made her feel sick. She went into the kitchen and filled a large glass with water. The cupboards were plastered with the kids' drawings. Sasha had to look away as their strange patterns jumbled and spiralled. She sat on the sofa and took tentative sips of the water. This wasn't the time for what the wine had left behind.

Sasha was still feeling dizzy when she wrote the text to Mike. He needed to know what had happened. Stan attacked? How? By whom? Was he going to be all right? Sasha disconnected his call when Mike rang a minute later. He was the last person she wanted to speak to – Mike with his logic and optimism.

"Dnt want 2 wake the kids by talking."

"Did Magda say how badly hurt he is?" Mike replied.

"Dnt know any more, will let u know what she says."

The house was very quiet. A tap dripped and the clock ticked. Sasha's pulse pursued a rhythm of its own as she wondered if the children knew. She thought of going to check on them but didn't want to be the one to wake them and have to explain where their parents were. On the rug, an unfinished Lego construction rested on top of its box. Bricks had been left scattered around it. Sasha picked up the pieces and put them back in the box. For a while she paced the room but her thoughts whirled faster than she could walk and her stilettos began to pinch. She kicked them off. After that, time moved in a laborious shift from one position on the sofa to another. She crossed and uncrossed her legs, alternating between leaning forward alertly and flopping back into the cushions. Sasha looked at each of the photos framed on the living room walls although she had seen them many times.

Her favourite sat on top of the television: a picture of the Jankowska family with Sasha, Mike and Jacob squashed in around them. It had been taken two months previously when Sasha and Mike had invited the Jankowskas over for a barbecue. Stan took several goes to set up the timer and run into place before the camera went off. Sasha thought it had probably taken longer because a lot of alcohol had been drunk that day. Stan's fruit cocktail hadn't lasted long and Sasha watched Mike become happier and calmer until all vestiges of the businessman had disappeared. As she and Magda talked their way through the warm timeless space of that afternoon, their husbands were having fun with the barbecue. Stan was watching Mike cook the meat, but by the time he started on a new box of lager, his competitive nature had come to the fore. Sasha looked up as Stan's baritone voice carried across the garden.

"Is that how long it takes you to cook a steak? I could've done five in that time."

Magda looked at Sasha. "Which crazy person brought him to the party?"

Sasha laughed. Mike was laughing too and telling Stan where he would like to stick his tongs. Stan nudged Mike aside and soon barbecuing the food had become a strange new sport. The boys were attracted by their fathers' game of who could brown meat the fastest. Sasha had been so relaxed by Stan's fruit punch that she didn't protest when he allowed the children a turn at the barbecue. After the meal, Mike dug out an old pack of cards and tried to teach the children Rummy. They had several good games around the table before Marcin's head slid onto Magda's shoulder and the family made to leave. The house had seemed very quiet with the party over and Jacob in bed. Sasha was scrubbing pans when Mike came to join her. He took the cleaned pots from her and dried them before putting them away. For a while they worked like that, a harmonious machine of routine and synchronicity.

When all the dishes had been put away, Mike said: "That was a great evening."

Sasha hadn't said anything because she knew she didn't have to.

§

Three hours went by before Sasha heard a car slow and stop outside. The poignancy of the memory of the barbecue lingered as she hurried to open the door. Magda came towards her with Stan a little behind. When he stepped into the lit hallway Sasha saw that one side of his face was bruised.

He grinned at her. "Sasha to the rescue. Thanks for that, by the way."

"No, it's… Are you all right?"

"I'm lucky." He allowed Magda to help him out of his coat. He was holding his right arm awkwardly. "Just a shame I'm not left-handed." The coat slid off, exposing an arm that was bandaged from wrist to elbow. "Right, time for a drink."

"Nothing strong," Magda said. "Alcohol stops the painkillers working."

"Leave the poor injured man with his vodka." He brushed against Magda on his way to the kitchen; she put out an arm to steady him. "If they don't work, I can take more."

Magda sank onto the sofa. "Have it with something then." Her eyelids drooped as she looked at Sasha. "Sorry. I didn't think we'd be so long."

Stan came to join them. "We had to wait hours for an X-ray. It's all the immigrants' fault, you know," he said drily.

Sasha assumed he would grin at her as he always did when he was being sarcastic. Now, he focused on the glass in his hands and the smile never came.

Magda was looking at the glass too; it was almost full of neat vodka. She put her face in her hands but didn't say anything.

Stan drank and seemed to be savouring the liquid. "And now, Sasha wants to know what happened." He put a hand up to the large bruise over his temple. "Right?"

Sasha nodded. The room felt cold and she folded her arms across her front for warmth.

"Well, I was on the train back from work and I was on the phone to my cousin in Poland. I don't know why, the signal was shit. Always is on trains. So it kept cutting out and I was swearing and these guys were looking at me."

"Were they sitting in front of you?" Sasha asked.

"No, across from me. Maybe I was being a bit loud and these men didn't like it. Anyway, the signal was fucking awful so we gave up in the end. The train was coming into Gloucester. I was nearly home. These guys started saying really bad stuff about me." The room was quiet as Stan took another drink.

"They said go back where you came from." Magda's voice was flat. "You don't belong here. The normal stuff."

"People don't speak to me like that," said Stan. "No one tries to tell Stanislaw Jankowska where I come from. So I told them. I was calm but they started going on about how I lie around all day on benefits. I told them I've just cleaned the floor of Great Western Hospital until it shines like you never seen. They said I deserve to have a crap job for coming here and stealing all the work. Well, they can say cleaning the hospital is crap work but they complain if I don't clean. That hospital must be cleaned and no one wants to do it. I told them that and I told them to fuck off."

"You didn't tell me that," said Magda.

"Sorry, but they can't just say what they want. These guys were drunk and it was like they were trying to say the worst things, you know? We were coming into Cheltenham so I stood up to get off. The next thing, I'm on the floor of the train with a station man standing next to me."

Sasha frowned. "So, these men, they…"

"They grabbed him." Magda spoke through her fingers. "He hit his head on the table. And it looks like they kicked him."

Stan grimaced. "It feels like it. They must have

stamped on me from the marks on my chest. They nearly broke my arm, fucking shits."

A slide show of horrible pictures was running in Sasha's mind. Stan grabbed by a group of faceless men. Stan's body being thrown about as if he were an object. Stan lying on the train floor.

Sasha watched Magda absently scanning the room; she recognised her friend's need to have something to do.

Magda's eyes settled on the Lego project on the rug. "What shall we tell the kids?"

Stan drained his glass. "Tata hurt himself on the train."

She walked across the room and picked up the model. "Jarek's not so young anymore. He will ask questions."

Stan yawned. "I had an accident on the train."

"There was nothing like an accident about it." She was playing with the topmost pieces of the construction. They sat in silence as Magda pulled bricks out and replaced them. Then she took out one of the large centre pieces and two of the walls broke apart. Magda looked like she was going to say something. Then she opened the box and put the Lego away, all destruction hidden from view.

She sat back down next to Stan and took his hand. "The police will be here in a few hours to ask us questions."

Stan nodded. He looked older and more serious than Sasha had ever seen him. "They will probably tell me that I shouldn't have got angry. I should have turned the other cheek, if that's what you say." He stood up. "I need sleep."

Sasha felt she should look away as Magda and Stan embraced. They held each other for a long time, Stan's right arm cradled against his stomach. Then he let go of Magda and headed for the stairs. Magda sat down next to Sasha.

"Aren't you angry?" Sasha asked.

Magda stayed silent for so long that Sasha wondered if she had asked the wrong question.

"I can't be angry," Magda said. "He's the angry one. The feeling… it's not angry. It's deeper. It's so deep…" Magda rubbed her eyes. "I'm so tired."

Sasha stood up. "I should go. Let us know if we can do anything, won't you?"

Magda showed her to the door. "Sasha, you're one of the best people I know."

§

The images of Stan's attack followed Sasha all the way home. Each time she turned a corner, she expected to find men waiting to kick her to the ground. She was relieved when Mike let her in, yet no sooner had she taken refuge in a kitchen chair and breathed in the warm safe smells of home than he was asking her about Stan. She cried as she told him, thinking all the while that Magda hadn't cried. Magda was by far the stronger, better person.

"I don't know what the world's coming to," Mike said. He spoke to Sasha from across the table but the distance seemed much greater. "I'll go and see Stan tomorrow. He's lucky, it could have been a lot worse."

It could have been a lot better too, Sasha thought. If those men had gotten on a different train. If Stan had got home safely. The world was spinning too fast. She thought of how Stan and Magda had reached for each other.

Mike's arms were resting on the table, a habit that usually annoyed her. His hands were tense, the fingers curved inwards. Sasha knew that he too was replaying the details of Stan's attack. She edged her hand forward as though to pick up her phone. Her movement dislodged the smell of the perfume she had sprayed on at the start of the evening. The scent had now faded so that the musk that made Sasha feel careless and free had almost evaporated. She moved her hand a little further forward. Her fingers were now centimetres from Mike's. He just needed to edge his hand a little to the left.

Mike stood up. "Would you like a cup of tea?"

Sasha shook her head.

"I suppose we should get to bed," he said.

She wished she could smooth away the tension in him, the way she had three years before when he came home with the news that he had missed out on the promotion he wanted. She had put her arms around him and stroked his back, creating creases in his shirt that were as faint as palm lines. She had ironed them out later, listening to his chuckles drift down the stairs as he bathed their son. The sound of Mike's laughter was more vivid to her because of the silence that now existed between them.

He was halfway across the room before Sasha spoke. "Mike?"

He stopped and turned back to her. "What?"

"You and me... We wanted the same things not so long ago."

Their eyes met. Sasha knew that Mike was trying to

understand her, the way he had always read her. Once he knew what it was Sasha wanted, he worked hard to provide it for her. Yet there had been many times when she wished that she didn't have to be so unsubtle about her wants, even after all their years of marriage. Mike was looking at her in the way a dog looks at its master, Sasha thought. He was waiting, and she wondered what clue she could give him. Her brain felt slow and tired. What was it she wanted?

Just as she thought this, Mike looked away.

On Leave

20 June 2016

Mike had taken a day's leave from the office. He hadn't told Sasha. The thought of her annoyance kept him quiet. He hoped to spend the day in the garden, pruning and trimming it back to its former neatness. Now, he was glad that he'd booked the time off because he had something else he needed to do.

Sasha frowned over his leisurely breakfast. Mike knew that she liked to have Jacob off to school and everything in the dishwasher by nine so she could start her day properly.

"Don't worry about me," Mike said. He pulled the butter towards him but saw that Sasha had taken his knife. Getting another knife himself would annoy her less than asking her for one.

She sighed as Mike opened the cutlery drawer. "You'll be late for work."

Mike crammed his mouth with dry toast to avoid replying. His teeth were clogged with seeds. Sasha had started buying "healthy bread" a few months before because she insisted it was better for Jacob. Mike wished she had remembered how much he disliked granary. He often forgot to put a loaf of white in the bottom freezer.

"You've not taken the day off, have you?" Sasha asked.

"Like I said, don't worry about me. I'll be out for most of the day."

Mike looked away from Sasha's clenching jaw.

"You should have told me. I've got people coming this morning."

"I'll be gardening, and I'll get Jacob at three."

Sasha scrubbed away at the sink.

A toast crumb prickled the back of Mike's throat, making his eyes water. "You still haven't heard from Stan and Magda, then?"

Sasha kept her back turned to him. "No."

"My texts to Stan still show as undelivered and I've just tried calling again. It went straight to voicemail."

Sasha looked at him properly for the first time that morning. "It's not like Stan to keep his phone off." She was wiping the same bit of work surface again and again. "Jarek and Marcin were already in the playground when I took Jacob to school. I must've missed Magda."

"She hasn't replied to me either. I'll go over now."

Sasha paused. "Maybe we should leave them in peace."

Mike screwed the lid back onto the marmalade. "We should see if they're OK."

"I'll go this afternoon," said Sasha. "I know you have to get back to work."

He had turned the lid so tight that he didn't know how anyone would open it again. "I want to see Stan."

Sasha reached across the table for Mike's empty plate. She gripped it hard as she said: "Send my love, won't you?"

§

Mike heard the safety chain rattling behind Magda's door before he had even knocked. He was accustomed to her flinging the door open and flooding him with exuberant chatter as she ushered him inside. Today, however, Mike was greeted by her frightened stare through the peephole.

"Who is it?"

Mike had never heard Magda sound so sharp.

"It's me. Mike."

Magda opened the door as far as the chain would allow. "Mike!" Her voice was breathy with relief. "Mike, it's good to see you."

The chain was scraped aside and soon he was receiving his usual welcome.

"Sorry I didn't reply to you," Magda said. "I've had my hands full." She came in for a hug.

Mike stepped aside as if to move out of her way before realising what she wanted. He felt an anxiousness that he couldn't place. Usually, their physical contact was normalised by the presence of Sasha and Stan, and their talk of the good time they would have together or the time they had just spent in each other's company. Mike's hug with Magda would last until Sasha broke apart from Stan. The men would look on as their wives chattered away and would have just started to talk amongst themselves when

Sasha would insist that it was time to move on.

Standing in the hallway, Mike and Magda embraced in silence. Magda was taller than Sasha and built like a tree. Mike saw faint shadows around her eyes and a smudge on her made-up cheek. Magda broke the hug.

"How's Stan?" Mike asked.

Magda turned away. "Not good."

Mike followed her inside.

In the sitting room, Magda curled into the sofa. "He's upstairs," she said. "He's been in bed all weekend."

Mike looked around. The armchair in which Stan tended to sit – usually with at least one child on his lap – was littered with Lego pieces, iPad balanced on one arm. Mike was used to Magda's chaotic attempts to clear space. Today, she didn't seem to notice that he had nowhere to sit. He stood awkwardly by the sofa for a few minutes before perching on its edge.

"He's in pain." Magda's voice was low and soft. "He won't tell you but I know. He has no… he doesn't want to do anything, you know? When he looks at me… sometimes, it's like I'm not here."

"Is there anything I can do?" Mike asked.

"I don't know."

"I was coming to see him. Do you think… Should I go up?"

"I don't know," Magda said again. "I'll go and ask what he wants." Magda stood up and Mike heard her uneven breathing. "I can't stop thinking about what they did. Why my Stanislaw? What did he do wrong? I keep thinking, are we so not welcome here?"

Mike reached out to… He didn't know what he was going to do. Magda grabbed his hand, reminding him of the way Jacob clung to him after a bad dream. Mike's thoughts seemed to be coming slowly; he felt as if he were watching something on telly, rather than taking part in it himself.

Magda's fingers closed around his thumb and she began to cry. "I'm tired, Mike. I'm tired." She sobbed so hard that she was struggling to stay upright.

"Come and sit down," Mike said. When Magda didn't move, he helped her clumsily onto the sofa. She fell into the cushions beside him and Mike stood up to give her space.

"I don't know what to say to the children. Their Tata is sick and they want to know why. Jarek asks lots of questions, so many questions. I think he knows and he's scared."

"Look," Mike said. He didn't know what else he was going to say.

"What should I do, Mike? What would you tell Jacob?"

"I would…" Mike couldn't think. "I always want to be honest with him, even if it's painful."

"Even if it's too painful?" She took a long breath and cleared her throat. "Sorry. I shouldn't be sad like…" She broke off.

Mike could hear footsteps on the floor above. He pulled his hands away. "Is he coming down?"

"Stan? He isn't coming down since he went to bed on Friday night."

They listened to Stan moving towards the bathroom.

"He knows you're here," Magda said. "I think he's just tired."

They heard the gurgle of pipes and feet padding back to the bedroom overhead.

"I should go," Mike said.

Magda was still crying. "I don't know… I just want this to be over."

Mike put his arm around her. Only Jacob needed him like this. Magda hugged him back, a tree swaying in the wind. He could feel her drawing on his strength; it had been a long time since anyone had needed him like this. Magda wasn't crying as hard now. He was making it better for her. She smelled of flowers and something like honey. Her hand was small in his. The bare skin of her arm was soft under his fingers.

Mike stood up a long time later.

"I think I'll leave Stan for now," he said.

§

When Mike reached home, Sasha was sitting at the kitchen table with Sarah, who came to cut her hair. They were chatting over cups of coffee; Sasha's newly cut bob bouncing with each nod or shake of her head. She looked around when Mike appeared in the doorway.

"Were they all right?" Sasha asked.

Mike nodded. He was about to tell Sasha how nice her hair looked but she had already turned back to Sarah.

Mike retreated to the garden. He breathed deeply but the air was too humid to be refreshing. He had almost walked the full length of the garden when he noticed the rose. It was badly overgrown, with spiky branches that protruded at child's face level. How could he have neglected it for so long? Times Past. Mike remembered planting it and felt a sense of loss when he remembered Sasha with the pot on her lap. He went to find the secateurs. As he pruned, the sun blazed on his face, as hot and intense as desire. Sasha's hair hadn't been as short since the day they'd met at that party. Now, it was almost as short as Magda's.

Inside Out

June 2016

Mike was used to the deserted state of the place, monitors fading to black around him as he continued to plough through project board reports and his ever-expanding inbox. He would be oblivious to the muttered "see-you-tomorrows" of departing teammates as he answered the emails till finally they pinged in less frequently, then stopped, and the chirruping of phones dwindled until the whirring of the aircon was the only sound in the office.

It was eight o'clock by the time Mike logged off. He sat back in his chair and rested his arms on the desk, conditioned air fanning the back of his neck.

It had been months since Mike had left at the same time as his colleagues; looking up to find himself alone no longer surprised him.

For the first month that Mike had decided to work overtime, Sasha left something in the oven or slow cooker for him. Mike remembered the day this stopped because she had sent him a text: "Found the pasta bake in the bin. Took me ages to make that. That's the last time I cook for you. BTW, Jacob would like to see his dad before his bedtimes."

Mike had intended to reply. He wanted to tell her that he just hadn't felt like eating that night, that she was the best cook he knew (including his mother, which was saying something) and that he should have thought to put the food in the fridge instead of throwing it out. He had ended with "sorry" next to a row of "xxxs". It would have taken him less than a second to press the send button but it wouldn't do any good, he told himself. He'd never been great with words and what he had just written was rubbish. So as it was, he spent three and a half minutes deleting the text character by character – ".ti yas ot woh wonk t'nod tsuj I uoy evol I" – until he was left with a blank screen and Sasha's words flagged in his internal inbox.

This evening was different because Mike had something to do between leaving the office and heading home. There had been constant reminders that today was an important day: his colleagues' mumbled conversations between meetings; Gav trying to lead him into discussion about the referendum before Mike could get him on task; the frequent vibrations of the phone in his pocket, bringing him notifications and news that was making the atmosphere in the office edgy and expectant. Now, it was Mike's turn to vote.

§

At St Paul's Church, everything seemed quiet. Mike opened the back door of his car and reached for his briefcase. His polling card was sitting on the top, slightly bent at a corner. He picked it up and went inside.

"Well, if it isn't Mike Glanford." Debra was smiling at him from behind the table. "I haven't seen you for ages."

"It's nice to see you." Mike hoped he looked like he meant it. "So, you're working at the polling station?"

"That's right." Debra looked smug. "I have to do my bit for the community." She took Mike's card. "We have to make sure these things are done properly, don't we?"

"I hope I'm not the only one to turn out." A feeble joke.

"Oh no, You're one of the last. I've been worked off my feet."

"I'll go and get on with it then," Mike said.

Debra held up a hand. "How's Sasha? I haven't seen her since we had that conversation."

"What conversation?" said Mike.

"Well, I know I can always be honest with you, Mike. I thought Sasha should know about what people are saying. She seemed a bit upset. I hope she's okay."

Mike wanted to know what she'd said to upset Sasha but he knew from experience that it could be a great number of things and that asking was what Debra wanted him to do. "She's fine." He made a move to go. "Well, I've had a busy day so I'd better get home before Sasha…"

"You spend a lot of time with your Polish friends, don't you?" said Debra.

So this was what it was about. "Yeah, I do."

"I heard about him getting attacked."

Mike resisted the urge to crunch his hand into a fist. "Did you?"

"It was all over the playground when I went to pick up the grandchildren. I feel sorry for those kids, but they don't really understand, do they?"

Mike shook his head. "Luckily Stan wasn't too badly hurt."

Debra leant towards him. "It just makes you think, doesn't it?"

He was puzzled by this.

"Well, if thugs like that can go for these foreigners, how safe are the foreigners' friends?"

Mike adopted the tone he often used at the office. "I'm not sure what you mean by that, Debra."

"Just that I would be careful who you talk to, especially these days." Debra had lowered her voice so that Mike had to concentrate to hear what she was saying. "Especially as... not that I should be telling you this." She looked around. "It's more than my job's worth to be... you know... but, put it this way, Mike. I'm getting a good idea of how this is going to end. The way people are talking, you know how it is. Better out than in, as they say." She pointed towards a booth. "Leave the pencil where it is when you've finished."

Mike wondered if it was worth voting after all, and then he couldn't believe he had thought it. He was getting as bad as Sasha, digesting everything Debra said without thought or objection.

Mike made his way into the booth and stood for a few seconds, trying to push what Debra had said out of his mind. He needed to concentrate on what he was about to do. Mike picked up the pencil.

His son.

Jacob.

Jacob's future.

Should the United Kingdom remain a member of the European Union or leave the European Union?

Can't we leave things to remain as they are?

Mike left a cross by Remain. He was in and out in five minutes, yet he would remember this moment for the rest of his life.

By the time he reached his car, the weight of Debra's conversation had returned to him. Perhaps she was just being her usual interfering self, or was there more to it? Sasha would know. He could ask her, but that would mean talking. She had been shaken by Stan's attack, leaving her with a fragility that was frightening to see. If he said the wrong thing, he felt she would come apart altogether, whatever that would mean. He might not know her as he had in their dating days, but he knew that Sasha kept going, whatever the cost to her… to them both. It was easier to stay quiet, Mike decided; he didn't want to give her anything else to worry about. She was friends with Debra, after all. Mike's stomach rumbled as he thought about all the cakes and biscuits Debra had made them over the years.

§

He'd driven halfway home – car windows down, shirt unbuttoned, tie removed and Jeff Lynne at full volume – when he decided to pop into The Exmouth for a drink.

He needed something that would cool and soothe the tongue. He waited in traffic, running through options in his head and imagining how each would taste. Yes, it was a lager sort of evening.

The pub was pretty full. The only table Mike could find was the one he'd once sat at with Sasha. It was a corner table, nicely out of the way. Mike took his first sip of vodka tonic and knew that he had made the right choice. He sipped the fizzy liquid and listened to the conversations around him: a group of women, deciding which club to start at; a family talking about their holiday plans on the big table behind; three men laughing at the fourth about his squash performance. Two older men at the table next to him:

"Did you see on the news? People have been going out in their wellies to vote."

"Typical British," said his friend, "and all them Glastonbury goers not realising they couldn't have their say."

"Not able to vote and covered in mud. Sounds like a damp squib all round. Do you think we'll get better weather if we leave Europe?"

They laughed before his friend replied. "This referendum had better not be a damp squib. Let's hope we make the right choice this time."

Mike took out his phone. No texts, an email about his energy bill, two Twitter updates and the time was 8.47. He opened his messages and selected Stan's avatar.

"At the Exmouth if you fancy coming out?" he typed.

A slice of lemon bobbed in Mike's glass, perversely

bringing to mind the image of Jacob's deceased goldfish floating in the toilet. Mike put his drink down as his phone flashed. He grabbed it but saw only the notification. Message failed to send. One of the men from the group nearby got up to order a round for his mates. Mike called Stan and was told that his phone was switched off. He typed Stan's home number in from memory.

"Hello?" It was Magda.

His words came out in a rush. "Hi Magda. Is Stan there?"

"Who is it?"

"It's Mike."

"Oh. Yeah, here he is."

A few seconds of silence.

"Hi mate," said Stan. He was trying to sound normal and it was painful. "I didn't think you would be on the landline."

"None of my texts deliver to you," Mike said.

"Dodgy signal, eh?"

"Your phone says it's off. How're you doing?"

"Not bad," said Stan. "You sound like you're in the pub."

"Yeah, I'm in the Exmouth. Want to join?"

There was a long pause before Stan replied. "Not tonight," he said. "I'm on bedtime story duty."

Mike wondered if Magda was with Stan as they spoke. He imagined her reaching for Stan, the way she had for Mike.

"Fair dos." Was his response prompt enough? Would Stan know what he was thinking about? Magda would have told him about what had happened; they seemed to be the sort of couple with no secrets or complications. Perhaps he was starting to see all couples that way.

"Did you go to the quiz on Tuesday?" Mike asked.

"I thought about it, but I was knackered after work, you know?"

"Yep, I know the feeling. I'm up for it next week, though. You'd better come, we need you for the history questions."

"Sounds good," said Stan.

"Sure I can't tempt you to come out?"

Stan laughed. "You can tempt me, but Magda's out so I have to get the kids to bed. Catch up soon though, yeah?"

Stan had hung up before Mike could remind him that Magda had answered the phone.

Mike scanned the menu on his table. Burgers, pie, fish and chips… His stomach clammed up at the thought of all that grease. What he would give now for Debra's chocolate orange cookies or her millionaire's shortbread.

I would be careful who you talk to, especially these days.

He would have to go home and tell Sasha. Mike downed his drink and left with a mouth full of ice.

§

Parking up outside the house, Mike saw that all the windows were dark except for a lamp in their room. It was usual for Sasha to go to bed once she had tucked Jacob in for the night. She would fall asleep in front of the TV and, being a heavy sleeper, it was easy for Mike to slip in beside her a few hours later.

During their engagement, Sasha had insisted on investing in a king-size double; "You can't have enough space," she had said.

Now this phrase returned to Mike like a motto when he dozed on his side. They never came close to touching.

The last six months had been a pattern of doing things for one another without seeing each other. Sasha would leave the door unlocked so that Mike could come in without fuss. Before he went upstairs, his job was to set the table for the morning: three spoons, two bowls, Jacob's dinosaur cup and bowl, Coco Pops and Frosties placed in the centre. Sometimes Mike would pull a box of cereal towards him, shovelling dry flakes into his mouth.

Today, he peered into the fruit bowl which also lived on the table. Atop a pyramid of apples and satsumas sat a large bunch of grapes. He pulled off one purple berry after another, cramming his mouth with their sweetness and rubbery skin. He threw the handful of stalks into the bin before he remembered Sasha's constant mentions of the compost. He considered rummaging through the rubbish to find the evidence of his thoughtlessness and then abandoned the idea in the hope that she wouldn't notice. He was light-headed from the heat and eating so much in a short space of time. The kitchen was warm. The windows had all been closed before his family had gone to bed. Mike was about to make his way upstairs when he heard the floorboards creak above him. He stopped, anticipating that the creaks would disperse in their familiar pattern towards the bathroom. He was surprised therefore when he heard feet on the stairs.

The door banged open and Jacob bounded into the room. Mike caught him just in time as he leapt into his father's arms. Jacob's hair smelled of Plasticene and Nivea. He buried his face in Mike's shoulder, putting several creases in his shirt. Mike's nose tickled. When he looked down, he saw that Jacob's pyjama top was on inside out and the label was rubbing against his skin.

"Mummy's asleep," Jacob whispered in his ear.

Mike put him down. "I know. You should be asleep too."

Jacob rubbed dust out of his eyes with his fists. "I'm not tired. I want to see stars."

Mike helped Jacob out of his pyjama top. "There won't be any stars now, It's only just got dark."

"I still want to look, though." His voice was muffled inside the garment.

Mike took the top and turned it the right way out. "The label should always go on the inside."

"Boring." Jacob was trying to open the back door, jangling the keys that hung there.

"Don't do that. You'll wake your mother," said Mike.

"I want to go outside," Jacob shouted.

"All right, we'll go and look at stars. But you've got to put this on first."

Jacob struggled as Mike pulled the top back over his head. Mike unlocked the door and his son ran outside.

In the dark garden, he watched the swing swaying

in the breeze. He heard a wind chime tinkling from a distance, eerie in the quiet. He smelt roses in the night air and turned towards the garden gate; the scent of Past Times was strongest in summer. Jacob went to lie in the middle of the lawn and Mike settled down beside him.

"I told you there wouldn't be stars," he said.

"I can see some."

Mike looked into the sky. "Where?"

"There."

"Where?"

"Up there."

Mike looked hard but all he could make out was the glow of a streetlamp in Pittville Park. He glanced at his watch. 11:13. The ballot counters had been at it an hour, reaching a conclusion paper by paper. Was Debra one of them? Surely not. Did Debra know any of them? A great tiredness fell over him like a thick curtain. "The universe is big you know, Jacob. It's very, very big."

Jacob didn't reply and Mike guessed he was asleep. Mike could almost imagine that the light he saw was from a nearby star, perhaps even a few stars. He thought of Jacob playing his space exploration games. The child's solar system consisted of infinite planets that supported human life – all planets that allowed Jacob to defeat the evil aliens. When Mike looked up into the sky again, he hoped the light was from Planet Lego and that it wouldn't go out.

§

Jacob and Marcin were standing over him, tall and padded in their spacesuits.

"We need your help, dad," said Jacob. Mike had to look closely at his helmet to see his son's small face behind it.

"What with, son?"

"This is Planet Debra and there's a really evil Martian here. We can't fight on our own."

"It sounds like a tricky planet," said Mike. "Luckily I repaired my space gun yesterday."

Marcin moved aside and the Martian stepped forward. It had a translucent face with thick veins under the skin. Its bulbous stomach was the raw pink of uncooked mince.

The Martian came towards him. "You don't belong here," it said in Debra's voice. "Go now, or I blast your little boy and his friend."

Mike raised his hand, willing it to turn into his space gun.

The Martian turned to look at him. "Do you love me, Mike?"

It had big eyes, Sasha's eyes.

§

Mike woke abruptly. His neck and back ached. It had been a long time since he had slept on hard ground. The birds were awake and something scrabbled in the hedge. Mike checked the time. 4:23. He turned his head and saw that Jacob was fast asleep. He didn't wake when Mike carried him indoors. Mike climbed the narrow stairs, thinking only of what was being uncovered around him. What was the outcome? He shivered as Jacob's foot brushed his arm; the child's hands and feet were frozen. In Jacob's bedroom, Mike tiptoed around trains and Lego figures and laid his son on the bed. He wrapped him in the duvet and slotted soft toys in beside him.

"Goodnight, son," Mike whispered. He was dogged by a feeling that he hadn't said enough and wished he could tuck his son in all over again so that he could say something else, something more profound.

A tinge of dawn showed through a gap in the living room curtains. Mike barely noticed as he flicked on the telly. He found he couldn't sit down and paced the room as footage of the night's events filtered into his brain.

Majority.

Nothing will change this result.

Was Sasha watching upstairs? Mike thought he heard something but when he muted the sound, he only heard telly fuzz.

Leave.

Leave.

Could he text Stan? Would he be awake? Mike imagined him and Magda holding hands on the sofa. Magda was wearing a lacy nightie that left most of her legs... Her skin had been so soft.

52 percent of the population...

His thoughts were making him feel sick.

Great Britain has voted to leave the European Union.

Mike retraced his steps upstairs, but this time he passed his sleeping son and went into his own room. "Sasha."

She was lying on top of the covers, her long dark hair falling over her chest.

"Sasha." The word came out as a croak. He wanted to touch her, to hold her hand, to wake her and say: "Sasha, It's bad news."

She slept with her thumb tucked inside her fist, just the way Jacob did. Mike couldn't bring himself to wake her. Instead, he took off his crumpled clothes and got into bed. Sasha moved in her sleep. For an instant, he thought she might wake, but she merely mumbled as she rolled over. She would know in the morning.

24 June

Sasha could remember the cause of their first argument almost a decade before. The first time she had stayed at Mike's, she had been woken by the loud beeping of his radio alarm clock.

"What time is it?" she had muttered, as Mike thumped the snooze button.

"Just before six," he said. "I set the alarm…"

"What?"

"Set it an hour early so I can… you know? Snooze it and still have time to…"

He had gone back to sleep. For the next twenty minutes, Sasha tried to get comfortable in Mike's single bed and block out the alarm that went off every five minutes. She had got up to find a cooler, quieter spot on his sofa, but the sofa was full of clothes he hadn't got around to putting away. She slumped in a kitchen chair, her doze broken by the sighing boiler and groaning fridge. By the time they sat down to coffee and stale cornflakes, Sasha was seething.

Since then, Mike's radio had been moved to the attic and the alarms to his phone. It had taken months of disturbed sleep for Sasha before Mike understood that the alarm didn't need to be set at full volume, especially not two hours before anyone else needed to be awake. These days, she was pretty good at sleeping through Mike's morning routine, although she occasionally felt the vibrations of his phone between dreams.

§

When Sasha woke up on 24 June, she had a strange feeling. It wasn't until she rolled over and elbowed something squashy that she realised that Mike was beside her, asleep. She tried to remember the last time she had touched him. She couldn't. It didn't matter, Sasha realised; she knew that something had broken.

Sasha reached for her phone. 8:36. "Shit!" She leapt out of bed, tried to dash in three directions at once and froze. "Mike! We've overslept."

His arm twitched.

"Quick, I need to get Jacob to school."

"Jacob," Mike echoed.

"And you're late for work."

No reply.

Sasha pulled on her dressing gown. "Do something."

Mike mumbled about how his phone must have died.

"So that's why the alarm didn't go off," Sasha said.

He didn't move.

§

Sasha threw the covers off a bewildered Jacob. "Wakey wakey. Hurry up, darling. We're late."

He sat up and rubbed his small sleepy eyes. By the time he had struggled out of his pyjamas, his lip had started to wobble.

"What's the matter?" said Sasha.

He shook his head.

Sasha took a deep breath to keep the impatience out of her voice. They didn't have time for this. "Tell me what's up."

"I'm late for school." Jacob's sobs seemed disproportionate. "I'm going to be in trouble, and Mrs Thompson will be cross with me and then Marcin won't play with me any more and everyone will laugh at me."

Sasha pulled him close. "I'll explain, and I'll write a note as well. I'll say it's my fault and you won't be in any trouble, all right?"

Jacob wiped his eyes on his sleeve and looked up. "Promise?"

"Promise," Sasha said. She wished she could start the day again just as easily.

Sasha had never understood why Mike liked to have the radio on over breakfast. She needed silence to wake up; he preferred a background of inane chatter. Mike was pouring coffee and buttering toast.

Jacob pulled at Mike's arm. "I want toast."

"That's not the way to ask," said Sasha.

"What do you want on it?" asked Mike.

"Jam and chocolate spread and no butter."

Mike's attention was focused on the Five Live

presenter. Sasha made to turn off the radio but he held up a crumb-speckled hand.

"You're late," she said instead. "Or are you on leave again?"

Mike shook his head. "I'm… ill."

"What's wrong with you?"

Mike took a step towards the radio. He hadn't heard her.

"Mike? Hello, Earth to Mike."

"I'm just listening…"

"You don't look ill."

"I'm not ill. I'm… I'll work from home."

"No!" Jacob screamed.

"Jacob," said Sasha. "Don't make that horrible noise."

"But It's got yucky butter on it."

Mike continued to spread the butter, as if he hadn't heard Jacob.

"Okay, I'll have that one," said Sasha. "Daddy will make you another one." Sasha lost patience. "I'm turning this off. I can't think with that racket."

"No," said Mike. "Sasha, the result, we…"

Oversleeping had put the referendum out of her mind. "We're still in, right?"

Jacob was jumping up and down in front of her. "We saw stars last night," he said.

She shoved bread into the toaster and her arm knocked against Mike's. "Did you, darling?"

"Yeah. Me and Daddy slept in the garden."

Sasha looked to Mike for confirmation, but he was standing next to the radio, a half-eaten piece of toast dangling from his hand.

"We saw lots of stars," said Jacob.

Mike turned the radio up.

Sasha poured milk onto Jacob's cereal, remembered that he wanted toast and hurried to retrieve it. She tried not to listen to David Cameron rambling on and on. Whatever he said, his confidence and privilege rankled.

"Why are we listening to this?" she said.

Mike turned the radio to its highest volume. Sasha looked down at the knife gripped tight in her hand. Jam dripped from its tip and pooled on the plate.

"We should be proud of the fact that in these islands we trust the people for these big decisions," Cameron said.

Trust him, Sasha thought. Mr Shinyface. And there was Mike, turning the radio up and up although it couldn't go any further than the end of the dial. Mike, oblivious and useless as usual.

"The British people have voted to leave the European Union and…"

"What?" Sasha felt the knife leave her hand but could do nothing about it. "Why didn't you tell me?" She wanted to shake Mike, to make him hear her. "Mike, you didn't…"

"I was going to," said Mike.

Jacob banged his empty cup on the table; the sound was louder and more jarring than anything in the room. "Finished."

"Go up and do your teeth," said Sasha, her mind already back on Cameron's speech.

"But I haven't had my toast," said Jacob. He looked like he was going to cry again. "And I want some more orange."

Jacob was saying something else, going on and on. Why couldn't Mike sort it out for once? And Cameron was still talking.

"I have also always believed that we have to confront big decisions, not duck them."

She had been ducking for weeks, ducking away from someone who worked and didn't do much else. In the pre-Jacob days, Mike had been someone she could rely on. If she asked him to do something, he did it. No questions asked.

Jacob tugged on her sleeve. "Where's my toast?" he shouted over the radio.

Sasha bent down, catching the honey smell of his hair. "I'll get it for you now."

"He's resigned," said Mike.

Sasha turned the radio down. "How long are we supposed to go on like this?"

"He's out," said Mike. "All those times I would have loved him to go and now…"

"We can't keep going," said Sasha.

"It's only just started," said Mike.

She laughed. "That's what you think. It's been like this for months, haven't you noticed?"

Mike took a step backwards. "Well, yes, it does feel like it's been on the news for—"

"I'm not talking about the referendum," said Sasha. Her voice was a cold, hard thing she didn't recognise.

"I know you don't want to talk about it," said Mike. "I'm sure lots of people feel like that but, Sasha, we've got to accept it somehow. We're out."

§

Mike stood at the bottom of the stairs and looked on as his wife and son walked out of the house. Jacob was telling Sasha something about his Action Men and didn't look around when Mike said goodbye.

"See you later, Sasha," he said.

She kept her back to him and closed the door behind her. Mike stayed where he was as the sounds of their footsteps and Jacob's babbling dwindled to silence. The house was quiet. A car drove slowly past the house and a seagull cawed.

Mike wasn't sure why he was avoiding work. He wasn't ill, although his body felt slow and heavy and he had a pain somewhere between his throat and his chest. Still, there was nothing stopping him driving over to the office now. It was common for colleagues to come in an hour late and make up for it at the end of the day. He imagined his team at their desks; would they wonder where he was? No doubt Gav would make some joke about him being hungover from the night before. They all knew that Mike had never been a clubber. Thinking about Gav made him want to stay away. He knew he couldn't avoid it forever, but he felt too old and tired to hear what they would be saying about the result.

He got his laptop from his briefcase and carried it into the garden. In the time it took to log on, he made coffee. There was no better way to work, Mike thought as he loaded up his emails. He breathed cool air deep into his lungs and felt himself relax. Eighty-three new emails.

Without reading any of them, he opened a new message and wrote in sick to his manager. The reply came back quickly:

"Sorry to hear you're not well. Rest up and hope you're better for Monday."

As he drank the last of his coffee, Mike looked around at the garden he'd worked so hard to cultivate. The lawn, once immaculate, was dented where Jacob's slide and climbing frame had stood. The grass grew in uneven tufts – evidence that it was now Snowball's domain. Mike looked towards the hutch in its corner between two walls. A pink nose was pressed against the bars; Mike wondered what she could sense in the air. The garden was overrun with dandelions. Mike pulled up a bunch and tossed them in the rabbit's direction. Loud crunching told him that Snowball was helping with the weeding. The largest flowerbed looked decidedly dishevelled, as if Jacob's space games involved trampling plants. And then there was the back garden and the patch of tall weeds that he'd been instructed to leave for "playing jungles". Jungles had been a nursery game, Mike remembered; Jacob was older and he hadn't realised. Despite his intentions when he'd taken the day off on Monday, he hadn't done anything with the garden. True, he had paced up and down and pruned a little here and there, but his thoughts had been on Magda.

§

Sasha still felt half asleep when they reached the playground. Jacob had stopped worrying about being late several roads back and Sasha tried to look as if she was listening to his elaborate explanation of his playtime games. Her thoughts replayed Cameron's speech. They were leaving Europe.

Jacob pulled at her hand. "Look, Mummy."

He was pointing at several parents, who were still standing outside. They seemed to be in a huddle.

"Don't point," said Sasha. "It's rude."

Sasha took a few steps towards them just as Jacob wriggled his hand out of her grip.

"Bye, Mummy," he shouted as he ran towards the school.

"Jacob! Wait." She jogged after him but soon found herself out of breath.

He had reached the door. "I'll be all right, I know where I'm going."

"Jacob!"

The door had already shut behind him.

Sasha was now level with the group; they were mostly women, some with buggies or a toddler in their arms. No one seemed to know where to look.

Sasha went over to one of the mothers. "Is something wrong?" she asked.

She gave Sasha an apologetic look and moved away with her pram. As she stepped aside, Sasha saw: "Magda!"

Magda was still, her head lowered and tears dripping off her nose. Something rose inside Sasha: a burning, aching strength she didn't know she could feel. She had to stand with her. "Magda, what's up?"

Magda didn't or couldn't reply.

Sasha held out her arms. She wanted to hide the strongest person she knew from the inquisitive onlookers. Sasha stayed like that until the shoulder of her cardigan was damp and her arms were starting to cramp. She heard someone whisper to the others about leaving them to it. Sasha heard them muttering as they walked away.

They had been alone in the playground for some time before Magda straightened up. Sasha thought she looked terrible, as if she hadn't slept for days. Without her smile, Magda looked twenty years older.

"Shall we go for a coffee or something?" said Sasha.

Magda blew her nose. "Thanks, but I should get back. Stan, you know?"

"I'll walk you home."

"It's fine, Sash, though, thanks."

"Is Stan worse?"

Magda shrugged. "Not worse, not better."

Sasha wished she had the words to say what she wanted. "I hate to see you like this," she said.

Magda's eyes filled. "The result, I hate it. It shows that I'm not welcome here."

§

Mike had no sense of time. He had mowed, trimmed, dug and planted until his back ached and his knees had seized up. He'd thrown aside his gloves when they became clogged with earth and dried leaves. Mike's fingernails were gritty, and his hands were rough and cracked, yet his satisfaction increased as the pile of greenery grew in the wheelbarrow. He only looked up when he heard his phone ringing. Berating himself for not taking it off charge sooner, Mike ran upstairs and grabbed the phone just as it stopped ringing. Missed call from Stan.

Mike called him back. "Sorry, I missed you."

"I guessed you're at work," said Stan.

"I've taken the day off," Mike said, "How're you doing?"

"I called to ask if you know where my wife is."

Mike swallowed. "No, I don't."

Stan laughed. "You sound so worried! I thought she might have got talking with Sasha and lost track of the time."

"What time is it?" said Mike.

"So you're the one losing track," said Stan. "She's not here since she took the boys to school." He was speaking with the same empty buoyancy as he had the night before.

It was making Mike edgy. "I haven't seen…" He broke off as he heard a sound downstairs.

"You haven't seen Sasha?" said Stan.

Mike heard the small squeak of the opening front door and realised he'd been holding his breath. "She's just walked in," he said.

"Oh great," said Stan. "I bet they've been shopping again. Stuffing their faces with cake somewhere when we're sitting here wondering where they are."

Mike laughed. "I think we're owed a pub night for this one."

"Too right," said Stan. "Anyway, I'm sure Magda's on her way. Speak soon, mate." Stan hung up.

Sasha didn't look up when Mike entered the kitchen.

"Everything all right?" he asked.

She had her head in her hands. Did that look all right to him?

"Stan just called me," said Mike. "He wanted to know if I'd seen Magda."

"She should have let me walk her home."

"From where?"

Sasha hadn't realised she had spoken aloud.

"Is Magda okay?" Mike asked.

"No."

"She's not? Sasha, has something happened?"

"Well, she's not going to be okay today, is she?"

Mike was standing close to her. Sasha wished he would move.

"I'm sure he'll ring again if she's not back soon." Was Mike thinking aloud too?

"She said she'd get Jacob from school," Sasha said.

Mike began rustling around in the cupboards; Sasha guessed he was making himself lunch. She lowered her hands. "Jacob can play there for a few hours, and she'll bring him back later." She picked up her handbag from the table. "I'm going to Tesco." She left the room.

§

Mike bit into his sandwich and texted Stan with a free finger: "She home now?"

Stan didn't reply until Mike was back outside, wheelbarrow emptied.

"Yeah, home now," it said. Smiley face. Mike tapped the grinning face wearing sunglasses, then the thumbs-up sign for good measure.

He was wheeling the barrow down the garden when he saw the rose. Times Past usually stood tall and proud, framing the gate with its fine pink rosettes. Now the heads hung down and the plant needed the gate for support. He moved closer, puzzled because he had pruned it a few days before. He could see that the flowers and leaves were covered in a white powdery substance. It was the worst case of mildew he had seen. Mike reached out and touched the flower. It was as soft as Jacob's skin had been as a new-born. A petal came away and fell to the ground. Mike picked it up and held it to his nose, seeking the strong, sweet scent that reminded him of summer. This petal smelled of cloying damp, like the attic when Sasha asked him to take things up there.

There was no part of the plant that the mildew hadn't touched. It would have to come out, the poor thing wouldn't recover. As Mike picked up his trowel, he remembered planting it. Sasha standing in the doorway, admiring what he had done. The way she had hugged him with the baby perched on her hip. How they had sat in the sun for the rest of that afternoon, entertaining the baby and talking about things that would occur far in the future. Their future. And all afternoon, they had shared the knowledge that if they didn't have the baby to occupy, they would have been inside, doing something quite different. Digging up the rose would leave a bare expanse of raw earth. He couldn't do it. Mike took up his secateurs and began to carefully cut away each infected part. When he stood up, only the long thorny stem was left with the last weak flower drooping from it.

§

They had almost finished supper – Sasha in the kitchen and Mike watching the news in the living room – when the car drew up. It was Sasha who answered the barrage of knocking at the front door. When she opened it, Jacob ran past without acknowledging her, Jarek and Marcin behind. She took a step backwards, just as Magda reached them.

"Sorry," she said, hugging Sasha. "Talk about making an entrance."

"Got you!" Marcin shouted, grabbing Jacob's t-shirt.

Jacob struggled free and threw open the back door. Sasha watched the children spill out into the garden. Jarek bowled Jacob over and sat on his stomach.

"Careful!" she called.

No one heard her. Sasha had never seen them play so roughly.

"They've been like this all afternoon."

Sasha turned to see Stan grinning at her from the doorway. "Stan!"

"Wow, don't hug so hard."

They broke apart.

"Sorry, I didn't know you were coming," she said.

"Someone's got to keep those boys in order."

"Have they been that bad?"

"Terrible. That Jacob Glanford, I blame the parents."

"Don't listen to him," said Magda. "Hey!"

Mike had come into the room. Magda went to greet him, but he moved towards the kettle.

"Time for a drink," he said.

The kitchen seemed cosy with the four of them together. Sasha knew that it was going to be one of those lovely evenings where they sat for hours, the children playing until they dropped and slept in a pack.

"Let's have something stronger," she said. "There's that champagne in the cupboard."

Mike gave her a strange look. "What's the occasion?"

It came to her instantly, as if it had been at the back of her mind all day. "Today's our wedding anniversary." She was looking at Stan and Magda as she said this.

"Nice," said Magda. "Congratulations."

Stan turned to Mike. "You tend to get more points for remembering your anniversary."

Sasha couldn't catch what Mike said in reply because Stan's laugh was loud.

"How's the arm?" she asked.

"Oh, fine," he said, flexing it. "And congrats, by the way."

"Thanks," said Sasha. "Let's go through."

"Wait," said Mike. "I've still got the news on."

Trust Mike to bring the news into it.

"No worries," said Magda, sitting at the table.

"Champagne's tempting," said Stan, "But I've got to drive."

"You're not staying?" Sasha asked.

The atmosphere changed as rapidly as if someone had squeezed the joy out of the air. Sasha felt a tightness in her chest that she couldn't dislodge. Magda opened her mouth to say something, but only shook her head.

"No," said Stan. "We're not."

Mike brought a tray of coffee to the table and sat down beside Stan.

"Good to see you, mate," he said, pouring drinks.

Stan seemed to be fascinated by the mug Mike was handing him. He cleared his throat. "Actually, we came to talk to you."

Magda looked away.

Sasha tried to swallow the dryness in her throat. "Is something wrong?"

"We're leaving," Stan said.

Mike was the first to respond. "What? Now?"

"We have been thinking about it for a while," said Stan. "And more after I was attacked. We're going tonight, we want it like that."

"Where?" Sasha's question came out harshly.

"First we're going to some friends. Then to Poland."

Sasha felt as she had the time she'd lost her footing on the stairs.

"Is this because of the referendum?" Mike asked.

"We're not welcome here," said Stan. "We know it now."

The back door opened and the children came in. They were no longer boisterous but tired and solemn. Glad of something to do, Sasha got up to fix them drinks.

Jacob stood between Jarek and Marcin. "Do you have to go?" he said as he did at the end of their time together.

It was when Sasha gave him lemonade that Jarek began to cry. He put the glass down and ran into Sasha's arms.

"Don't cry," she said, trying hard not to cry herself.

"It's not fair," said Marcin.

Jarek closed his fingers around Sasha's. "Can you come and see us in Poland?"

"Of course we will," said Mike. "It will be a nice holiday for us."

"When?" said Marcin.

"Soon," said Stan. "We'll make it soon."

Magda got up and helped herself to a piece of kitchen roll. She was about to sit back down when Jacob flung his arms around her legs.

"You're not going," he said.

"Don't be silly, Jacob," said Sasha.

"You're silly," he shouted.

Stan checked his phone. "We've got to go soon," he said. "We want to be in Birmingham by eight."

Jarek was a heavy weight on Sasha's lap, adding to the sense of being pressed down upon.

Stan stood up. In all the time they had spent together, this was the first time Sasha had seen Stan with nothing to say. Mike stood with him. Magda was moving towards the door with Jacob still wrapped around her.

"Quick," said Marcin. "Come on, let's hide."

"It's a bit late for that," said Stan.

Sasha would never know how she got through the goodbyes that had once been their ritual, and now signified the end. They were saying too much, they were saying too little. There was nothing that could be done to slow time or make it less painful. She watched Mike prize Jacob from Magda and hold him close, their son ferocious in his misery. She followed Mike outside as Magda and Stan bundled the children into the loaded car. Without looking back, Stan started the engine and drove away.

§

As soon as the car was out of sight, Mike put Jacob down and he ran for the stairs. He guessed the child had gone to seek solace in his battalion of Action Men and the other distractions his bedroom provided. He knew that Jacob could recover from their friends' leaving more quickly than he and Sasha would. Sasha stood beside him, staring at the place where the car had been. He wondered if she was sharing his wish for it to reappear, Magda apologising for having forgotten something. Or perhaps Stan would come bouncing towards them, laughing about how their leaving had been a wind-up; he'd been trying to get him back since Mike had stolen his phone and changed the names of his contacts. Sasha made a small sound. Glancing over, Mike saw his hopelessness reflected in her bowed head and blank eyes.

For the first time in many months, Mike put his hand out to Sasha. Perhaps minutes went by, or maybe it was a mere second or two. Then, she moved her hand closer to his. In the gateway to their garden, where loping shadows darkened the work Mike had done and a faint scent of Times Past lingered on the breeze, Sasha and Mike turned towards each other as their fingers touched.